Murder Trouble

By Louis Trimble

Originally published in 1945

Murder Trouble

Published by Resurrected Press

This classic book was handcrafted by Resurrected Press. Resurrected Press is dedicated to bringing high quality classic books back to the readers who enjoy them. These are not scanned versions of the originals, but, rather, quality checked and edited books meant to be enjoyed!

Please visit ResurrectedPress.com to view our entire catalogue!

For updates on future releases, LIKE us on Facebook:
http://www.Facebook.com/ResurrectedPress

ISBN 13: 978-1-943403-40-0

Printed in the United States of America

RESURRECTED PRESS BOOKS IN
ERIC LEVISON'S
DR. EDWARD LESTER MYSTERY SERIES

Hidden Eyes

Eyewitness

Ashes of Evidence

RESURRECTED PRESS BOOKS IN
H. ASHBROOK'S
DETECTIVE SPIKE TRACY MYSTERY SERIES

The Murder of Cicely Thane (1930)

The Murder of Stephen Kester (1931)

The Murder of Sigurd Sharon (1933)

A Most Immoral Murder (1935)

Murder Makes Murder (1937)

Murder Comes Back (1940)

Murder on Friday (1941)

RESURRECTED PRESS BOOKS FROM *THE ETHEL THOMAS DETECTIVE STORY* SERIES BY CORTLAND FITZSIMMON'S

The Whispering Window

The Moving Finger

Mystery at Hidden Harbor

The Evil Men Do

RESURRECTED PRESS CLASSIC MYSTERY CATALOGUE

Journeys into Mystery
Travel and Mystery in a More Elegant Time

The Edwardian Detectives
Literary Sleuths of the Edwardian Era

Gems of Mystery
Lost Jewels from a More Elegant Age

Anne Austin
One Drop of Blood
The Black Pigeon
Murder at Bridge
Murder Backstairs

E. C. Bentley
Trent's Last Case: The Woman in Black

Ernest Bramah
Max Carrados Resurrected:
The Detective Stories of Max Carrados

Agatha Christie
The Secret Adversary
The Mysterious Affair at Styles

Octavus Roy Cohen
Midnight

Freeman Wills Croft
The Ponson Case
The Pit Prop Syndicate

J. S. Fletcher
The Herapath Property
The Rayner-Slade Amalgamation
The Chestermarke Instinct
The Paradise Mystery
Dead Men's Money
The Middle of Things
Ravensdene Court
Scarhaven Keep
The Orange-Yellow Diamond
The Middle Temple Murder
The Tallyrand Maxim
The Borough Treasurer
In the Mayor's Parlour
The Saftey Pin

R. Austin Freeman
The Mystery of 31 New Inn from the Dr. Thorndyke Series
John Thorndyke's Cases from the Dr. Thorndyke Series
The Red Thumb Mark from The Dr. Thorndyke Series
The Eye of Osiris from The Dr. Thorndyke Series
A Silent Witness from the Dr. John Thorndyke Series
The Cat's Eye from the Dr. John Thorndyke Series
Helen Vardon's Confession: A Dr. John Thorndyke Story
As a Thief in the Night: A Dr. John Thorndyke Story
Mr. Pottermack's Oversight: A Dr. John Thorndyke Story
Dr. Thorndyke Intervenes: A Dr. John Thorndyke Story
The Singing Bone: The Adventures of Dr. Thorndyke
The Stoneware Monkey: A Dr. John Thorndyke Story
The Great Portrait Mystery, and Other Stories: A Collection of Dr. John Thorndyke and Other Stories
The Penrose Mystery: A Dr. John Thorndyke Story

The Uttermost Farthing: A Savant's Vendetta

Arthur Griffiths
The Passenger From Calais
The Rome Express

Fergus Hume
The Mystery of a Hansom Cab
The Green Mummy
The Silent House
The Secret Passage

Edgar Jepson
The Loudwater Mystery

A. E. W. Mason
At the Villa Rose

A. A. Milne
The Red House Mystery

Baroness Emma Orczy
The Old Man in the Corner

Edgar Allan Poe
The Detective Stories of Edgar Allan Poe

Arthur J. Rees
The Hampstead Mystery
The Shrieking Pit
The Hand In The Dark
The Moon Rock
The Mystery of the Downs

Mary Roberts Rinehart
Sight Unseen and The Confession

Dorothy L. Sayers

Whose Body?

Sir William Magnay
The Hunt Ball Mystery

Mabel and Paul Thorne
The Sheridan Road Mystery

Louis Tracy
The Strange Case of Mortimer Fenley
The Albert Gate Mystery
The Bartlett Mystery
The Postmaster's Daughter
The House of Peril
The Sandling Case: What Would You Have Done?

Charles Edmonds Walk
The Paternoster Ruby

John R. Watson
The Mystery of the Downs
The Hampstead Mystery

Edgar Wallace
The Daffodil Mystery
The Crimson Circle

Carolyn Wells
Vicky Van
The Man Who Fell Through the Earth
In the Onyx Lobby
Raspberry Jam
The Clue
The Room with the Tassels
The Vanishing of Betty Varian
The Mystery Girl
The White Alley
The Curved Blades

Anybody but Anne
The Bride of a Moment
Faulkner's Folly
The Diamond Pin
The Gold Bag
The Mystery of the Sycamore
The Come Back

Raoul Whitfield
Death in a Bowl

And much more!
Visit ResurrectedPress.com
for our complete catalogue

FOREWORD

Murder Trouble is an example of a type of American mystery that evolved out of the hard-boiled detective stories of the 1920's and 1930's. These mysteries, though they may feature their share of mayhem, are not as dark as their predecessors. Taking a cue for Dashiell Hammett's *The Maltese Falcon* and *The Thin Man*, there is a lighter touch to the plotting and the dialog is snappy and sarcastic in tone. The central characters are not professional detectives, but individuals who find themselves caught up in some criminal affair, usually a murder, where they become the chief suspect.

As with the hard-boiled detectives, the path out of their troubles is achieved not by the patient sifting of clues, but by stirring things up until the real culprits reveal themselves. Unlike the detectives of the hard-boiled school, though, they manage to succeed not by their skill with their fists or guns, but by the quickness of their wits. The appeal of these amateur sleuths is that they represent everyman and not some iron jawed hulk.

Murder Trouble, published in 1945, is set during World War II, but except for rationing and the black market, the war action makes little intrusion into the story. The central figure, Tom Hallam, is a former San Francisco reporter, who after spending an extended time in a hospital for lung trouble, takes a job on a small town weekly paper in Washington state looking for less stress and fresh air. Of course, that is now what he finds. Instead, he finds himself caught up in a murder mystery complete with a voluptuous but deceitful blonde, a federal agent and assorted crooks, characters, and bodies.

This type of mystery is essentially an escapist fantasy. The hero finds himself in an impossible situation, surrounded by diabolical villains and beautiful women. As the prime suspect, his very existence is threatened. He bounces around from one adventurous episode to another until finally overcoming all obstacles to unmask the true criminals, and usually get the love interest in the end. Given this, it is not surprising the Trimble that would turn to science-fiction in his later career.

While Louis Trimble is better known today for his academic work and science-fiction novels, his mysteries were well-written and entertaining. It is with pleasure that Resurrected Press presents this new edition of *Murder Trouble*.

About the Author

Louis Preston Trimble (March 2, 1917-March 9, 1988) was an American author and educator. Born in Seattle, Washington he worked as a house painter and a logger before joining the academic staff at the University of Washington as an instructor and later professor of the humanities and social sciences. His academic work looked at the role language plays in science and technology. His career as an author began with the sale of a short story in 1938. Over the span of thirty five years he wrote in a variety of genres including mysteries, westerns and science fiction. His mysteries include titles such as *The Surfside Caper* and *You Can't Kill a Corpse*.

Greg Fowlkes
Editor-In-Chief
Resurrected Press
www.ResurrectedPress.com

I.

It was one of those cold, dark days with a hint of snow in the low, flat clouds. The road curved down into a canyon of pine-forested walls and then zoomed to daylight again on the crest of the hills.

It was good-looking country; from the crests I could see endless miles of low, forested hills stretching to Canada. Every now and then there was a flash of water, little lakes huddled among the trees.

I was taking it all in between glances at the deserted road and my speedometer, held at an almost patriotic forty. Looking off that way at the scenery I almost missed the big car pulled up half on the road and half on the narrow shoulder. I swung out to avoid it and just caught a glimpse of a man in uniform bending down by an outside rear tire. I put on the brakes and then backed up.

The car was a big Cadillac, maroon-colored like my own small convertible. It looked as long as a train and much more prosperous. The uniform turned out to be a chauffeur's outfit. I backed parallel to the man in it.

"Help?" I asked.

He looked up. He was handsome in a smooth-featured way. His eyes were a little too small and pale but I could just imagine the women swooning over the curve of his lips. Right now they were set in annoyance.

"Quiet," he said in husky whisper. "You'll wake Mr. Burnham. He's ill."

I looked in the rear of the car and had a glimpse of a huge bulk in a fur-collared coat, a moonlike face set in placid lines of sleep. A scarf was drawn high around Mr. Burnham's chin and a Homburg low over his forehead. He looked much too comfortable to let a little conversation disturb him. But the chauffeur's tone irritated me.

"Okay," I said.

"Besides, I'm nearly finished," he added.

I nodded, shifted into low and pulled away. I let the matter slip from my mind and concentrated on my weak financial condition and the state of my gas tank. It wasn't too strong, and I had six weeks to wait before my next coupons were valid. I was hoping I hadn't skinned it too closely when I had figured this trip. It was nice country but not the kind I would care to be stuck in.

Another couple of miles and the Cadillac passed me with a soft swoosh. Mr. Burnham seemed still to be asleep. The chauffeur made no move to indicate he recognized me. There was none of the cheery wave of the hand so common among motorists. He drove with his eyes straight ahead, both hands on the wheel. My only satisfaction was in thinking how much gas a big motor like that used.

I was just beginning to enjoy the scenery again when the hitch-hiker popped out at me. It was a girl and she jumped into the road and waved her hands up and down. I had to swing out to keep from hitting her. I slammed on the brakes and turned back toward my own side of the road and finally stopped on the hard dirt shoulder. She came running up, an overnight bag swinging from one hand.

"For God's sake," I said, "were you trying to commit suicide?"

She had the door open and was climbing in. "I was trying to get a ride," she said in a husky voice. She was panting a little from her sprint. "I don't want another night in those damned woods."

She was a tall girl and when I managed to get a good look at her I saw that she was close to being beautiful. She wore an expensive looking black and white slack suit with a grey cloth coat on top. The coat was open and the suit clung nicely to her more prominent attractions. She wore nothing over her head and there was a metallic glint in her blonde hair that hinted of strong rinses. That and a noticeable hardness in the lines of her face were the only things that kept her from being really beautiful. But it was nothing to kick about; it wasn't very often that a hitch-hiker turned out to be anything approaching her. I watched her settle herself with the little suitcase on the floor beneath her feet. I knew it wasn't supposed to be healthy picking up hitch-hikers, particularly in wartime, but I was a sucker for anyone on foot. Pedestrianism is one trait I have never developed successfully.

"I'm going to Letsburg," she said. "And what a time I've had trying to reach that town!" She leaned back. After a moment she dug into her coat pocket and came up with a pack of cigarettes. "Smoke?"

I had the car going again. "I have some in the glove compartment," I said. She put her own away and got mine out. She lit two and handed one of them to me. I took, it hoping she wasn't bothered with pyorrhea.

"If Letsburg is on this highway I'm going through it," I said. "I'm heading for a place called Vinson. It's somewhere in these parts."

"Vinson-oh!"

I didn't care for the way she said it. "If I don't like it I'll keep on going," I said defensively. Like hell I would— but it was none of her affair that I was short on money and shorter on gas.

"There isn't much to like," she said. "Nothing to the place—unless it's trouble."

"What kind of trouble?"

Her voice had the effect of a shrug. "I don't know. Just things you hear."

I let the subject drop and soon she started talking again. I listened half-heartedly. I was thinking of what she had said and wondering if I had recovered my usual ability to get myself into things. The two years I had spent in the sanitarium had given me a taste of peace and quiet and I was beginning to like them.

"The bus ran into a blizzard," she was saying. "It hit a ditch and left us stranded in the middle of Idaho. I got tired of waiting around and after it stopped snowing I got a ride on a truck into Pullman. A farmer took me as far as he could and dumped me. That was ten miles back. I've been waiting for a ride all night."

She said it all at once, got through with it, and stopped. Later I was to wish I had exhibited some curiosity and asked a few questions, but it didn't seem either important or exciting to me, so I muttered the necessary sympathetic remarks and let it pass.

After a while we topped a rise and dropped into one of the prairie valleys that dot the northeastern part of Washington. The hills were timbered about halfway down their slopes and then the land was barren the rest of the way down and all along the valley floor. Plots of winter wheat and frozen cabbage plants covered the dark soil, and in the center of the valley a fair sized town squatted around a meandering creek. Pretty soon a sign on our right announced, "Letsburg, Population 4217." There were a number of Kiwanis and Rotary signs rather badly in need of paint and finally the town itself.

"Where to?" I asked her.

"There's a hotel farther down the line," she said. She finished her second cigarette and crushed it out in the ashtray. She was rubbering out of the window, but without looking directly at her I couldn't tell if it was a new sight or if she were hunting for old landmarks.

When we reached the county courthouse she scooted over a little closer to me. This, I thought, was a hell of a time to get friendly. Or was she figuring on making a touch, maybe having me stand her hotel bill? I was just the kind of sucker who would, and platonically, and so when I saw the hotel sign announcing rooms from one dollar I felt a little less worried.

But she let it go at that until I pulled up in front of the two-story frame building. She opened the door and got out, hauling her little suitcase after her. "Thanks, Tom," she said.

That stopped me. I blinked at her like a fool. She

laughed. "You are Tom Hallam?"

"Sure, but—"

She didn't wait for me to finish. She leaned inside and kissed me casually, and then backed out again. As she closed the door I heard her voice. It was quite loud. "Do hurry, darling."

I jerked the car into gear and left Letsburg. I didn't know what the gag was but it made me sore. Not that I minded being kissed by a good-looking woman, but I couldn't make out what she meant by that last remark, nor did I get it how she had known my name.

I glanced down at the registration certificate clipped around my steering post. It was facing the other way, to the left, so she couldn't have picked it up from there. I had uneasy feelings that I tried to stifle. The last thing my doctor had said when I left his sanitarium was, "Take it easy, Hallam. You can't live like you used to. Fresh air and quiet and you'll be good for lots of years. Stay out of trouble."

There was plenty of fresh air around but I wasn't so sure any more about the quiet. The thought of working on a weekly newspaper hadn't appealed greatly to me when I had first received letters from the Vinson Record, but it seemed to fit the doctor's orders, so I had accepted the offer of a job and started north. And the first thing I had run into was someone who seemed to regard Vinson and trouble as synonymous.

To hell with it, I thought. The world was full of screwballs. That kiss and last remark had been her idea of humor, and as for knowing my name she must have read my registration certificate somehow.

I wasn't satisfied but it was the best I could do, so I concentrated on the landscape again. There were a few more dips and rises and then the road branched. A signpost pointed north to Canada and west to Vinson, seven miles, and Seattle, three hundred and seventeen miles. Seattle was beyond my reach for a while, but it was a place to head for if I didn't like Vinson. I took the turn and followed the road up and down until it finally took a graceful curve down to a little town plunked between steep, tree-covered hills.

It was surprising. There was no warning, no population sign. There weren't even the usual highway signs inviting me to stay at this place or that and be sure to eat at so-and-so's beanery if I didn't want indigestion. There was just the white road tunneling through the trees and then the solid brick buildings of the little town and around them a few frame houses surrounded by partly cleared fields. I counted five brick buildings in all and not more than twenty-five houses. If the mileage sign hadn't been at the junction I might have gone right through the town.

The first brick building on my right as I entered the town was one-story and from the looks of its windows had been a drugstore. There was a vacant lot, then another building across whose windows was lettered "VINSON RECORD." Across from that was a two-story brick with a swinging sign over the porch announcing itself as the HOTEL VINSON. I coasted on a way.

On closer inspection the other buildings turned out to be a grocery store, looking pretty well cleaned out, and a general store that was closed. The frame houses all had one thing in common. They were white frame and New England architecture. I found the inevitable school and church, both with towers and bells. It was incongruous, New England away out here. But was it? There were pine forests and hills. The setting was right; I wondered about the people.

I reached the edge of town and made a U turn to have another look at the hotel. The tiny town fascinated me. I would have shuddered had anyone used the word to me, but it was best described as quaint.

The hotel sign had smaller lettering underneath the name. "Gateway to Paradise," it read. "Monthly rates."

"While waiting for St. Peter to make up his mind," I

mused. But I stopped. This was it. Paradise might be over the next rise, and again it might be out of range of my gas tank. And experience had taught me a hundred dollars lasted longer in small towns. Besides, I had a job here if I wanted it.

II.

The interior of the Vinson Hotel was of dark mahogany that looked as if it had been aged long before it was shipped around the Horn. The walls were mahogany-panelled and the majority of the furniture was of the same stuff. Outside it was gloomy enough, but in here it was even worse. The big stone-manteled fireplace that covered nearly one entire wall held no fire and the ancient pot-bellied stove set in the center of the room was as dead and cold as the air around it. In all that huge lobby there was no one, no life but myself. No bellhops, no clerks, not even lights.

I went up to the big front desk and looked for a buzzer of some sort. All I saw was dust, a thick layer covering the mahogany surface.

I began to feel scared; a little chill had crept through my overcoat and was making itself felt on my skin.

"Hey!" The room boomed the word back and sent it echoing off into lonely corridors.. I tried it again. "Hey!" Not hotel etiquette perhaps, but neither was having the front doors open so a guest could walk into desolation.

I held my breath, my ears searching for some sound. I heard it. From out back came a steady thumping. It grew louder until I could recognize it as the sound of a man walking—unnaturally. And when he came into sight, appearing suddenly from a dark areaway, I saw that the thumping had been caused by a peg leg.

I almost laughed aloud. For a moment the combination of chill and gloom and the eerie sound of the thumping leg had almost brought me to believe in the stories of haunted houses. Then on top of it this ghostly-looking man with a wooden stump for one leg appeared.

He was as close to a ghost as I ever want to come. He clumped toward me, looming larger and more grotesque. The color of his eyes was hidden by the gloom and his thick white eyebrows. But there was no mistaking the search of his gaze. His face was dead white, set under a thin fluff of white hair. His face was wrinkled and the wrinkles had set his features in a perpetual scowl. He was huge, inches taller than my six feet, and his breadth made my beanpole build look even skinnier.

When he was within five feet of me he stopped and looked down at the suitcase in my hand.

"Closed!" he said. His voice was raspy and querulous; ridiculously small coming from such a behemoth of a man. "Closed tight."

"You mean you're out of business?"

"Closed for the season," he announced. His face did not change expression. It just looked sour. "Come back next summer." It was not an invitation; there was no graciousness in his manner.

Season? What season, I wondered. But season or not, I had to have a place to stay. "All I want is a room. A quiet place. I don't need any service."

"Closed tight until summer," he repeated. His voice held such finality that I nearly gave up. But a natural persistence plus an unreasoning irritation at this unpleasant old man kept me trying.

"Are you the owner?"

"Nope."

"Can I talk to the owner?"

"Won't do you any good." He rubbed his chin with a thick, white hand. "Over to the *Record* across the street."

I presumed he meant the owner. A fine hotel, where the head of it had to work in a small-town newspaper office to keep things going. "Thanks," I said tartly.

"Won't do you any good. We're closed till summer."

That refrain was beginning to annoy me. I nodded shortly, turned around and headed outside. A stray snowflake hit me as I reached the bottom of the steps. I squinted into the sky. The flakes were idle ones, coming only now and then, but it was growing darker and the air had the heavy feel of a storm on its way. I was certain I wanted no part of driving in a snowstorm in this semi-wild country.

I dropped my bag into the car as I passed it and then went into the *Record* office. I was prepared to use every argument I could lay tongue to. But all of my priming seemed unnecessary. When I stepped inside the newspaper office it was almost as deserted as the hotel. A long counter stretched from one side to the other, cutting off the front from the rear. I could see darkness-enshrouded hand presses deep in the back of the room. There were three desks just beyond the counter. Only one was occupied. A cone of light from a green-shaded bulb flooded down on the lone occupant, a girl.

I let the door close a little harder than was necessary. "I heard you," she said without looking up. She got through whatever she was doing and then rose. She walked to her side of the counter and smiled at me.

It was quite a smile. Just seeing it made me feel that my stop had already been worthwhile. You couldn't call her a beautiful girl. The best word I can think of is willowy. She was very slim and the slightest bit round-shouldered. She had hips, but not in back—that went down as straight as a man's. She wore a tight-fitting grey wool dress with bits of green on it here and there. The dress showed that she was flat-stomached, but she had nice lines. Her breasts were easily her most outstanding characteristic. She looked about twenty-seven, but her figure was as youthful as that of a girl ten years younger.

She wore glasses on a rather broad, intelligent-looking face. Her features taken individually would have stopped no clocks, but collectively they blended into a pattern so odd that it was just short of being lovely. Her nose was small, her eyes big and set a little too far apart. Behind the glasses they looked as gray as my own. Her cheek-bones were high and her face narrowed from them to a heart-shaped chin. Her mouth was a good deal too big and on it was the only make-up she wore, a slash of red. She wore her hair in a loose knot at the nape of her neck and it looked good to see long hair again. It had started out to be red hair, but had given up and stayed a soft gold with but the faintest sheen of auburn where the light caught it right. That was all right, I thought; two red-heads aren't supposed to get along so well.

The whole effect of her was one of serenity, of quiet and capable loveliness. I had a hard time putting my finger on a word for it, but at last I got it. She was interesting-looking.

Her smile stayed while I gawked. I recovered myself and went up to the counter. "My name is Hallam," I said. "Tom Hallam. That means nothing to you but it's a start."

The smile went out. "If you're T. D. Hallam, it means a lot to me," she said. Her voice had the softness I expected, only I got the impression that she was suddenly ill at ease. She shifted nervously behind the counter.

"Guilty," I admitted.

"Then you did decide to take the job. I was so afraid you wouldn't—that they might draft you or you'd die or something." She didn't sound as pleased as her words indicated. I don't mean she objected to my presence, but it was much as if my arrival had sent a last forlorn hope glimmering. I got that impression despite her lip service to me.

"Not much chance of my being drafted," I said. "And they let me out of the sanitarium because I wasn't ready to die." I didn't care for the subject, so I continued, "By the way, before I talk about a job, I want to see if I can get a place to stay. Is the boss here?"

"Boss? I'm the boss," she said.

"You're the one who wrote me! You're E. L. Vinson?"

"Guilty," she mocked me.

"An old ghoul in the hotel across the street told me I'd find the hotel's owner here. Is he about?"

"Yes," she smiled. The way she said it tipped me off.

She laughed at my expression. "I'm that, too," she said. "This town is my baby. The paper and the hotel, all of the brick buildings, and six hundred acres of highway going in both directions. None of it's worth anything now, but I like it."

"And you run the newspaper too?"

"I write it, set the type, and print it. I even take it to Letsburg and mail it."

I felt funny inside. I had jaunted all the way from California on an A card to find myself face to face with a one-woman newspaper. And I was supposed to work for her! Working for a woman was a matter of prejudice; I had never actually done it. There was some consolation, though, in the thought that she was good-looking in a nice, bosomy way.

"You didn't found the town too?" I asked, trying to smile at her.

"No," she laughed. It was a very nice laugh. Like wind in fall leaves or water over a tiny rapids. "No, my grandfather did that. It burned in '98 and he and Dad rebuilt it. They owned the bank—we haven't one now— and they built the stores of brick and most of those little New England houses as well. Grandfather came from Boston around the Horn and he refused to allow any other type of architecture here. I like it.

"Anything the matter with my owning a hotel?" she added.

"Only that it's an unusual occupation for an attractive woman," I said.

"I've been to the city, stranger, so keep the line to yourself," she said. But she didn't sound displeased. After a moment she added, "I'm Eve Vinson and I do own the hotel."

"I hope," I said fervently, "that the old man I so injudiciously called ghoul wasn't your—"

She chuckled. "Hardly," she interrupted. "My father is dead. Adam is what they would call the family retainer in the East. And he is odd-looking."

"Adam?" This time she was kidding. Adam and Eve!

"Actually," she assured me. "Eve is Adam's wife's name. I was named for her. I really think that's why they married—because of their names. Only there isn't any confusion. Everyone calls her Bossy."

The reason for that became obvious after I met Adam's wife. It was all a nice personal touch and possibly an interesting Sunday feature but it wasn't getting me any place.

"Adam tells me you're closed for the season," I said.

"That's right. We used to stay open winter and summer. But we don't catch the tourists coming up for the ski season since gas rationing started. And I haven't the fuel to keep the place comfortable in winter. Nor the energy to wrangle over food points with the O.P.A."

"Fuel, with this forest?"

"And no one to cut it," she reminded me. "So I stay open in the summer now and get a few of the old trade coming here for fishing or on their way to the National Parks. I'm sorry."

"I could stand a lot of things," I said, "but no heat isn't one of them. Cigarette?" I offered her my pack. I was surprised that she accepted. I started to light one for myself, too, and then remembered the doctor's orders. I put the cigarette back and got out my pipe. I wasn't supposed to smoke cigarettes at all; I only carried them because a pipe was a nuisance while driving. A pipe, he claimed, was more healthful. It should have been more satisfying—it certainly was more trouble.

I waited until her cigarette was going good and tried again. "What I want is a place to work and sleep," I said. "One room is all I need. Quiet, so I won't be disturbed and won't disturb anyone. I have a folding typewriter table and the snappiest collapsible chair you ever saw. With those and a bed I can hole up for the winter between dashes to this office. Is there such a place in town?"

She looked thoughtful; then she smiled. "Do you do fiction on the side, Mr. Hallam?"

"Hardly," I said. "Fiction is out of my line. I'm still a newspaper man—in a way. I'm free-lancing features and occasionally news stories. And every now and then I run into material for a true detective—that sort of thing." I grinned a little wryly. "My old sheet in San Francisco is very charitable."

"It's not charity to pay for good writing," she said indignantly. "You have a defeatist attitude."

Boom, like that I was psychoanalyzed. "So have you," I gibed. "You let the O.P.A. close you without a wriggle."

There were two spots of red in her cheeks. Then she laughed instead of getting sore. "You can't get me to open the hotel that way," she said. "But I do know of a place you might use."

"Lead me to it—if there's a stove."

"Only one thing," she said. "It's haunted—literally."

Which was a queer thing to say to a prospective employee who needed a place to stay. Especially when her letters to me had been almost pleading in asking me to come and work for her.

III.

I had the city person's amused tolerance for small-town people. And when I saw my haunted quarters my amusement increased. And since I was more or less at the mercy of the small town so did my tolerance.

The place was in reality a two-room house. Or one large room divided by a high partition. The building was of white frame like the other houses in the town. It sat just behind the hotel, between it and a long, ancient carriage shed that faced the plowed fields and spurs of forest. One of the spurs, in fact, angled around the carriage shed and came to the very edge of the little house. A pathway led from the hotel, split halfway to the carriage shed. One branch of it went to my place, the other straight ahead. The split was marked by a quite small but freshly painted old-fashioned privy. It even had the half-moon cut in the door. My house—I already regarded it as that, and before long I was going to put up a fierce fight for the right of possession—was perhaps twenty feet from the privy.

Eve Vinson opened the door of the house and led me in. She found a string dangling from the ceiling, jerked, and a good strong bulb threw the entire interior into bright relief.

"One thing we have is electricity. This place isn't furnished with an electric plate for cooking, but I can get you one."

I was looking around happily. "I have my own two-burner," I said. "This place is really something." It was certainly more than I had asked for. The main room was about twelve by twelve with a wood range and a sink against the far side. Cupboards were above and below the sink and on the sides. Along the right wall, set in the space between two large windows, was a drop-leaf table and four chairs. Across the room were davenport, easy chair, floor lamp, and an odd chair. Beside the front door was an empty bookcase.

The other room was a bedroom, with a curtain over the aperture that led into it. There was an old-fashioned high bed with a tall headboard, ornately carved. A marble-topped dresser and one chair. One corner had been curtained off to form a closet. The room wouldn't hold any more.

"I'll do more than rent this," I said fervently. "I'll buy it and live in it through my declining years."

"It has drawbacks," she said. She was obviously pleased with my reaction. "It's really part of the hotel—a sort of guest house—though few have used it. None for more than one night."

Fairy tales again! Haunted houses. Certainly, though, Adam was ghostly enough to fit into the story. "Any other drawbacks besides spooks?"

"There's no hot water," she said. "The stove has a reservoir on the side. Your water for dishes and such comes from it. It's a good stove and will heat the room as well as you want. And the plumbing is that little house we passed at the fork in the path. It's a long twenty feet on a cold winter night. So—" She stopped, reached under the bed, and drew out an old-fashioned thundermug. "And don't think you won't be glad to have it."

"What do I bathe in, the sink?"

"If you're accustomed to it," she retorted. "But there's a tub and shower in the hotel. Adam, Bossy, and I live in the back. You're welcome to a bath any time you wish."

She lived not fifty feet from me; a nice neighbor, I thought. Not to mention the most palatably landlady I would ever have.

"And," I said, "this is complete with haunt for how much?"

"Why!" She looked at me and laughed a bit self-consciously. "I don't know—by the month. Oh, say ten dollars."

"My paper in San Francisco isn't the only place dispensing charity," I said stiffly. "That wouldn't pay for the electricity, to say nothing of the wear and tear."

"It would—really." She didn't seem put out because of the crack I had made. Possibly she was humoring my more metropolitan conception of prices. Small towns, I found later, thought ten a month quite a good rental, especially in off seasons.

I said, "Okay. I like it. And if you have no objections I'll pay it in advance for a few months."

"None," she said. "If you change your mind or prove a bad tenant and I have to toss you out you can have your money back." She smiled brightly. "You also can have this end of the carriage shed for a garage. That pile of wood alongside it, by the way, is for you to use too."

I nodded and turned toward the door. It was cold in the little house. The dead cold of disuse. I wanted to get unpacked and start a fire in the stove. She followed me out, closing the door behind her. A few vague flakes of snow hit us in the face.

"There's a key somewhere," she said. "I'll see if I can dig it up for you." She added almost apologetically, "We don't use keys much here."

"I won't worry then," I said. "Now how about a restaurant and a grocery store?"

"There's a better restaurant than in Letsburg," she said. "It's the truck shop on the west edge of town. Ike's place. But our grocer is about out of business. We go to him for meat and emergency things; otherwise we go into Letsburg. People here take turns shopping for the others. It saves gas that way. The drugstore is in Letsburg too. Ours was drafted along with the doctor. We have a veterinary for emergencies." She laughed at my obviously shocked expression. "This is an unincorporated town," she said. "If you count all the farms in the district and add the men who've been drafted you might get close to two hundred people."

"Post office?"

We were walking along the broad veranda that stretched all the way around the hotel. She gave me a quick look and a laugh. "The mail comes through once a day and is dropped at the hotel. I take it over to the newspaper office and hold it for those who want it. But 'most everyone maintains a box in Letsburg."

In spite of the sound of things I was beginning to feel a fascination. The place should be good for a few features and a rest, if not for crime stories.

"And now," I said, "we can go into the Record, and I'll pay you; then we'll see about the job."

We had rounded the side of the hotel and were starting down the steps to the street. In front of the Record office was the big maroon Cadillac that I had met on the road. I knew it was the same car because when we got close to it the obese Mr. Burnham was still snoozing in the back seat.

The chauffeur was inside the office. He had his hat off and I saw now that he had wavy blond hair. His features looked more than ever like the kind women go for. I scowled at him. I hoped Fatso and this guy weren't going to stay here too. I wanted no competition from a man who looked like this one; my slightly battered profile wouldn't stand a chance. All I had to offer was a too thin six feet, red hair, and a face that told of K. of C. smoker fights as a kid south of the Slot in San Francisco. And my weak chest.

This man was too handsome and he looked as if he might be intellectual. Eve Vinson seemed the kind of girl who would enjoy that.

He took no notice of me. He moved toward her, limping a little, and made a half-bow. A mocking sort of bow, I thought. "Miss Vinson?"

"Yes?" She was rigid, staring at him. I looked quickly at her. There was a flush on her high cheekbones and her hands were clenched tight. It was as if she were afraid of him. But by the way they spoke neither knew the other. "Yes," she said again. "I'm Eve Vinson." The tension began to ease out of her as she waited.

His voice, when he spoke again, was melodious in a hand-trained sort of way. "Mr. Burnham," he nodded in the general direction of the Cadillac, "regrets that he can't speak to you but he is worn out from the long drive. He is quite ill, you know."

I felt better after hearing this line of mush. It evidently exasperated Eve Vinson. "I didn't know," she said spiritedly. "And who is Mr. Burnham?" She was staring straight at him. He stared back, a little quirk of a smile on his handsome mouth.

"Mr. Prigwell's executor," he said. He sounded as if she should know everything now. "Here are the papers." He drew a long, fat envelope from his pocket and handed it to her. "Mr. Burnham has business in Letsburg, should you wish to communicate with him." He bowed again, that same way, and limped out. Eve stood and stared at the envelope until the big car drove out of sight.

She walked to her desk and half collapsed into her chair. "I'll be damned!" She made it sound good, necessary. It wasn't coarse and forced as some women sound when they swear. "And what is this?" She looked at the envelope, then at me. "I don't—I don't know who Mr. Burnham is, nor Mr. Prigwell!"

I liked her more and more. Her explosive words sounded fine coming through those vivid red lips. "You have me," I admitted. I went to work signing three of my traveller's checks over to her. "I didn't like that guy when I saw him before," I commented. "I liked him less this time."

She swivelled in her chair. "When you saw him before?" Her eyes were big.

I didn't see anything to get perturbed about. "He was changing a tire. A few miles the other side of Letsburg," I said. "I offered to help and he very nastily declined any."

"Oh!" she said. She tried it again, "Oh!" The second

time she made it sound casual.

I gave her the three checks and she dropped them into her purse without looking at them. Her whole attention was riveted on the envelope. She slit it open. There seemed to be a sheaf of papers and held to them by a paper clip was an easily recognizable object. The paper clip popped off and it fluttered to the desk top. It was long and green, a check. She read something written on the papers and then picked up the check.

She looked at me. "A check for two thousand dollars," she said. "The first installment on my inheritance." She was shaking her head. "I seem to be Mr. Prigwell's heir! Me!" She looked closely at me.

It didn't mean anything to me, but she seemed to expect something. I registered surprise.

"That's nice," I offered.

She got up suddenly. I liked that; the gray dress was a nice, close fit. "Nice! I never heard of Mr. Prigwell!"

IV.

It was damned puzzling. I chewed it over in my mind all the way to Letsburg. I had made arrangements with Eve Vinson about the job and then had gone about the business of getting settled. There was no rush to start work, she informed me. Only that morning she had taken the papers into Letsburg and mailed them.

Letsburg loomed up before I realized it. I glanced at the mileage on my speedometer. I had noted it before I left and now I saw it was just a little over twelve miles from one hotel to the other. I drove slowly up the brightly lighted main street, looking for the inevitable chain grocery store. There was one just across from the courthouse. The parking lot was full so I turned into it, backed around, and parked across the street under the bare trees fronting the courthouse.

When I got out of the car three men were crawling from the one ahead of me. It was a V-8 sedan with official plates on it. The smallest of the men was holding the others back and when I stepped under a street light I saw that he moved toward me a little. The other two followed closely.

"Well, hell!" he said. They had reached me now and I saw that the one who had spoken was unknown to me. He was a small man, with a sharp face and a little stubble on his cheeks and chin. He wore disreputable slacks, a turtle-neck sweater and a cap pulled low on his head. His voice was nasal. He looked like a person who would use "dese" and "dose" but it really came out almost cultured.

"Tom Hallam!" he said. "Here, Sheriff, this man can identify me."

I must have looked as puzzled as I felt. The big, blocky man standing on the left of the one who had addressed me said, "You know this man?"

"I never saw him before," I said.   I made it sound as if
I meant it. The word sheriff had been enough to frighten
me off. I wanted no trouble.

"Your name Hallam?"

"Yes," I replied. "He may know me, but I don't know
him."

"Hey," the small man said, "this is no time for a gag."

"You'd better come along," the sheriff told me. His
voice was like the deep roll of the sea. "Formality."

"For what?" I demanded.

"Check; routine," he answered. "That's all." He bobbed
his shaggy head at the courthouse. He wore no hat and
the snow flecked thickly in his hair. I didn't argue with
him. There was no point in it. Besides, he was much too
big.

After we got into the basement offices of the
courthouse and he shucked his overcoat he was still big.
Tall and thick all the way through. His hair was pale
yellow shot with grey, his eyes were a washed blue. He
looked like a Finn and he said his name was Saarkinnen.
He knew my name, so he introduced me to the third man,
who had been silent up to now.

He was a little smaller than I, but round and buttery
with a very dark skin and black, shiny hair. His name
was Morozzi. He looked me over carefully.

"Know him?" the sheriff asked.

"No," Morozzi said. "Never saw him before."

We all sat down, the sheriff behind a neatly littered
desk. He looked mildly about. "Let's get at it."

"Like I told you," the small man said. "I came here on
business. To meet a man. He hasn't showed up yet. It got
cold and started to snow when I was out walking—killing
time. I went into that chicken house for protection. It was
a dark day. I thought they'd be asleep. How did I know
chickens would squawk like that?"

The big sheriff grunted. His eyes turned to me. They
were mildly amused. "Okay—you."

I told him briefly of myself, where I was staying, and

why. He nodded and finally stopped me.

"This gentleman," he said to me, "is registered at the hotel under the name of Ralph Burnham. His wallet contains cards identifying him as Joseph Prigwell. I found him in a chicken house at the Morozzi residence. He was digging a hole in the ground."

Burnham! Prigwell! Were those two names going to start haunting me? I looked with fresh curiosity at Burnham-Prigwell.

"I was killing time," he repeated. "Aw, look. I got excited when those chickens started cutting up. Maybe I kicked one too hard. I'll pay for it. I was trying to bury it before I got caught—that's all."

Saarkinnen grinned. "I've heard all kinds of stories but that is the best. He takes a walk, it starts to snow, he goes into a chicken house for protection. The chickens fly at him. He kills one by accident. What must he do? Bury it; hide his guilt. Spade is at hand and so he digs a hole." He stopped.

"Damn it," Burnham-Prigwell shouted. "It's my story. Take it or leave it. I'm a citizen. I have some rights. I want those rights."

"When they start wanting rights," Saarkinnen observed softly, "then I smell something."

Burnham-Prigwell just grunted. Morozzi looked at him and then at the sheriff. "Maybe he is telling the truth," he suggested. "But transients have stolen my chickens so often lately." He sounded mild and apologetic.

"Like hell," Saarkinnen said. "Anyway, I'm going to hold him, John. Come in tomorrow and we'll see what we've turned up."

Morozzi spread his hands. "I have to be in Lewiston day after," he said. "I'm leaving again tomorrow."

Saarkinnen made an allusion to travelling salesmen and how sorry he felt for their wives. It escaped me since I wasn't up on local gossip. Then his smile dropped as he turned from Morozzi to me.

"Do you know who this man is, Hallam?"

"I told you I didn't," I said.

"Hell," Burnham-Prigwell said. "It was in Frisco."

"You lived there?" I asked him.

"Sure. And you used to work on the *Mail*."

"Like hell he lived there," I said to Saarkinnen. "Only outsiders ever call San Francisco 'Frisco'. I did work on the *Mail*. I was in the Press Room at the City Hall for a few years. Maybe that's where he saw me." I didn't usually like to turn the heat on anyone, but I wasn't going to get myself in a jam for this man. I didn't know what the stir was all about. Burying a dead chicken didn't seem much of an offense to me, but evidently the sheriff thought differently. Which made me all the more determined to keep my nose clean.

"Maybe," Saarkinnen said, "I'll wire Frisco—San Francisco—and see if he has a record."

"Go ahead," Burnham-Prigwell said calmly. "It's a waste of money, but go ahead."

I stirred in my chair. "Look," I said. "I have a twelve-mile drive to make and it's snowing. And I have to get some groceries before the stores close. How about letting me get started? You can check up on me all you want. I'm not running away." I grinned. "Take a look at my gas ration and you'll see that I can't."

Saarkinnen seemed to believe me. But he grunted something about a matter of routine and reached for the telephone. He told the operator to get him the Vinson Hotel. There was a long wait and he took a plug of tobacco from his coat pocket and bit off a chew. It was well started when the telephone came to life.

"Eve? This is Saarkinnen." He cocked his head away from the phone and spit into a cuspidor somewhere on his side of the desk. I heard the shot ring metal. "I have a Thomas Hallam here. He says he's working for you. I'm just checking—routine. No, he hasn't done anything that I know of—yet." There was a wait. "Okay, Eve, you bet." He hung up, spit again, and turned to grin faintly at me. "You can go."

I left them. The last I heard was Burnham-Prigwell objecting strenuously that he wasn't getting his rights. A few seconds after I reached the top of the stairs leading up and outside I heard footsteps and Morozzi caught up with me.

"Let Saarkinnen have it," he said. "Sorry you got rung into this. I think the man is crazy myself."

He seemed a harmless, mild sort of guy. "That's okay," I said. "It was a little diversion." If, I thought, the sheriff didn't decide to look me up now every time a chicken was missing.

"Forget it, will you?" Morozzi asked.

"Forget it?"

He nodded his butter-jowled face. "It'll just cause gossip. There's too much now."

"Sure," I said. "It's forgotten." He smiled and turned away. I saw him hiking off through the snow, heading home I supposed.

I walked across the street to the grocery store. I got all the things I wanted. Unlike in larger towns, there seemed to be plenty of meat. I had plenty of ration points, so I had quite a spree buying everything I wanted. By the time I left and got the stuff into my car I was close to being broke. Still, I felt pretty good. I had talked the grocer out of half a case of beer.

The shopping had taken me nearly forty-five minutes. I hurried. The main thing I wanted was to get back to my little house and nice, snug fire I had laid with my own hands. I couldn't get it off my mind. I wondered if I were going to turn into one of those satisfied, settled people to whom life is all warm houses and firesides. That would be a laugh.

"Getting old, Hallam," I told myself. That was all right with me. The way I felt now I could settle down and write those two book-length political essays I had been planning. Sure, and starve to death—I was about five miles out when the incongruity of making a living off that kind of writing struck me. I had to laugh at myself. Well, maybe I would marry Eve Vinson and settle down to run a small-town paper forever.

Not a bad idea, and I plowed on through the snow getting nice mental pictures of her in the tight, gray wool dress. I was feeling pretty well set up by the time I rounded the side of the hotel and headed for the carriage shed. The snow was a lot heavier and I was glad to get the car under shelter and start for the house. There was a soft yellow light spilling out of the windows at the back of the hotel. The snow fell soft and fat and thick through the light squares. It looked nice, peaceful. No matter how I came out I didn't want small-town cops and a chicken burier named Burnham-Prigwell cutting in on my mood of peace.

That's what made it such a shock when I pushed open my door, snapped on the light, and nearly stumbled over the body.

V.

It was a man; he lay on his back, his arms outstretched and his terror-wreathed features staring upward at me. His head lay in a pool of blood. His eyes were open; they stared glassily. It didn't take any knowledge to know that he was dead. Nor any to see what had killed him. A thick, foot-long length of stovewood lay just on the edge of the pool of blood. It was reddish brown on one end. The pool of blood was hardening too in the chill air.

I felt dazed at first, uncomprehending. The naked light bulb cast harsh whiteness over the body until the very starkness of it made me realize what had happened. That clicked something in my mind. Too many years I had seen murdered men, men dead of hundreds of accidents, looking in death at dozens of horrible sights. Realizing that this was a man and that he was dead, murdered, brought an automatic response to my mind and muscles. I took a closer look at him. He was in his early forties, a man who in life would have been described as small and wiry. His face was thin, too.

His hair, what I could see of it, was thin and dark; he wore a small black mustache and the faintest pretense of a goatee. His clothes were extremely well cut. They looked expensive and conservative. The palms of his hands were smooth and unlined and looked as if they had always been that way. No manual labor for this man. The soles of his black, high-laced shoes were so new I could see the make on the leather beneath the arch.

I looked around the room. And I began to notice things that set my backbone tingling with implications. The ashtray by the davenport contained the ashes and butt of a cigar. Looking more closely, I found the cigar band and cellophane wrapper of a well known fifty-cent corona. A glass ashtray I had not known I possessed sat on the other arm of the davenport. It had what looked to be fresh ash and bits of charred black in it. But any butts that might have been there had been removed. I noticed, too, faint damp spots on the thin carpeting all the way from the door to the davenport. Some were quite wet—the melted snow I had brought in. Others were almost dry, barely splotches on the rug; those this man had carried with him. This man and another; the two ashtrays made me certain of that.

Obviously he had not killed himself, so there must have been another with him. It wasn't that over which I puzzled, but the idea that there was a conversation, a period perhaps, where two people relaxed, smoked, and chatted before one rose, got a piece of my stovewood and then applied that same wood forcibly to the skull of the other.

I looked at my woodpile. It seemed smaller than I had remembered. I went to it. I sniffed. I lifted the front lid of the firebox. Inside, instead of the neat arrangement of paper, chips, and small logs I had left, was only blackened ash. It had evidently been a short fire and a quick one. I could lay my hand on the top of the stove and feel only the faintest warmth, and the room still held a chill.

But it explained something that had puzzled me. Why didn't the dead man display an overcoat and a hat? And rubbers on his expensively shod feet? He was the kind of man who would wear rubbers. I looked at the feet again. They showed no signs of water such as would be left by melting snow. So, unless he had flown in, he had worn some kind of rubbers.

Automatically I put away the groceries I had bought with so much enthusiasm. I wasn't feeling exceptionally brave, but I forced myself to grope through the curtain and into the dark bedroom and stab my hand through the blackness until I found the light dropcord. I pulled and prepared to duck. Then I felt silly. There was no one there.

I peered under the bed; I pulled back the drapery that formed the front of the closet and looked in there. I stepped back and looked again. "I'm going nuts," I thought. "I need a drink."

I left the bedroom and went to the kitchen cupboard in which I had stored my little hoard of beer. The bottles were nicely chilled from the drive home. I took my knife out of my pocket and pried open the blade that has the bottle-opener on it. There never was a knife invented that was so handy to open things with as a boy scout knife. Only boy scouts don't, as a rule, use them on the same things I do.

I drank from the bottle, letting the faintly cool liquid gurgle pleasantly into my stomach. When the bottle was empty I felt better, much better. I liked beer; and the doctor had recommended it for my weight. What more could a reasonable man ask?

Then I went back into the bedroom. I looked in the makeshift closet again. The things were still there. A neat gray overcoat and, on a hook, a darker gray felt hat. It was a Homburg like the fat Mr. Burnham's. But there were other things. Two dresses; a woman's suit. A gray tweed suit, and the dresses were warm wool ones: one a dark, reddish brown and the other a deep, lustreless green. They looked like small sizes. My eyes traveled downward. There were the rubbers on the floor and next to them a pair of woman's galoshes, white, and next to those a pair of black pumps.

"Jesus!" I backed out and looked wildly around me. There was no one there. Who then had put all these clothes here? And why? I looked under the bed again to make sure. Nothing but my two suitcases. I jerked open the bureau drawers. I had a good idea of what I would find, but it was a shock just the same.

In the top right-hand drawer I had put my underwear

and socks, in the left I had crammed my handkerchiefs, extra gloves and muffler and my shaving equipment. In the middle drawer were my pyjamas and shirts and the bottom drawer I had reserved to use for dirty laundry. But now the right-hand drawer held underwear, socks, and handkerchiefs, and the left was filled with neatly folded lingerie. I jerked some of the stuff out. Weblike brassieres; diaphanous lace-trimmed pants of mauve and green silk. I looked in the second drawer. My shirts and pajamas enjoyed the company of my gloves, muffler, and shaving stuff. The bottom drawer yielded a sheer white blouse, two extravagant-looking slips, and the most exciting and useless appearing pair of green satin pajamas I had ever seen. And tucked away in a corner was a pair of hose.

One thing struck me about all of the feminine apparel, even the dresses and shoes. It looked as if it had never been worn. All but the hose. They were of sheer silk, filled with ladders and with holes worn in the toes and heels. They didn't look so very large. I examined the shoes. They and the galoshes were size five. I hunted in the dresses and suit. There were no labels, but I judged them to be small sizes—about twelves or fourteens. The lingerie looked about the same.

All that hunting for identification marks reminded me of my corpse. I legged it back into the front room. He was lying as I had left him and he didn't look any better. I still shuddered when I looked at the grisly mess, but years of training were with me and I could stand it. But I took a deep breath and held on when I knelt beside him and began exploring his pockets.

I found nothing. No wallet, no papers, not even a handkerchief. His suit revealed no more. There were not even labels in his clothes. I didn't look in his trousers; I drew the line at stripping him. But I did look in the overcoat and hat. There was the make in the hat but none in the coat. It looked, as did his suit, tailor made. Obviously   then   there   should   have   been   some identification by the tailor and, more likely, the man's own initials in his clothing.

Someone, I reasoned with little effort, had decided to keep me from identifying him. I turned away to get my own coat and hat and only then did I realize I hadn't taken them off. Shrugging, I left them on while I built another fire. Only this time I thrust in paper and threw wood and chips on top. To hell with being careful if someone else was going to get all the benefits of my artistry.

That done, I lit the fire and went outside. The snow had lightened and it felt a good deal colder. I pulled my coat more closely about me and made tracks for the yellow squares of light that meant the back of the hotel. I tried to tell myself I wasn't afraid, but there, in the blackness of a country night, every shadow was darker and bigger than any the city ever offered. I ducked them all and by the time I reached the back steps of the hotel I was almost running, and I could feel myself sweating. I hammered at the door.

Eve Vinson opened it. I was glad at the moment I didn't have to face the ghoulish countenance of Adam. It would have been a little more than I could take. She snapped on a porch light.

"Oh!" she said. "Is everything all right, Mr. Hallam?"

"Shouldn't it be?" I asked warily.

She gave me an odd look. "The sheriff's office in Letsburg called and I thought—but come in. I'm rude." She held open the door, shivering a little. I went onto a screened-in porch and then into a big, white-walled kitchen. It was warm in there and the sound of water boiling came from the huge wood range.

"Tea," she said, following my gaze. "I'm making some. Will you join us?"

"I don't know," I said. I looked at her. She was still lovely in that odd way. I felt comforted by being with her. Her serenity was as soothing as a drink of whiskey after a strong shock. "I'm not sure." I felt I was babbling;

reaction setting in. It had always done that to me. After I
was away from the core of a story I always had periods of
incoherency until my mind was readjusted.

"Are you ill, Mr. Hallam? You sound—" Then she
smiled. "But perhaps the misunderstanding with Sarky
made you nervous."

"Sarky?"

"Mr. Saarkinnen, the sheriff. He's really nice. We call
him Sarky. He doesn't mind."

Misunderstanding was a nice way of putting it—and
of feeling me out. "It was a mix-up," I conceded. "But it
isn't that. Miss Vinson, I'm afraid you were right. The
house is haunted."

She looked startled, then nervous. "I've heard Adam
and Bossy claim—but—" She stopped and stared at me.

I went on as calmly as I could. "But there's no mystery
about the haunt. The body is lying on the front room floor
now—freshly dead."

It was a damned fool thing to do, I suppose. If she
hadn't been made of strong stuff she would have fainted.
She swayed a little and then stared at me, her mouth
trying to make sounds.

"A dead man in there. . . .Who?"

"I don't know. I can't find out." I hit the words hard.
"And there are drawers full of women's clothes in the
place. Nice new lingerie. Two dresses. A suit, shoes,
galoshes. In mauve and green with lots of lace." I don't
know why I said it that way unless I was still incoherent.
Certainly it must have sounded wild.

She looked at me a long time, then smiled. It wasn't
much, but she did smile. "Mr. Hallam," she said
soothingly, "come in and sit down."

"Damn it," I said, "I'm not drunk; I'm not crazy. Come
and see for yourself." I found I was shouting and lowered
my voice. "Sorry—I'm excited. But if you have a strong
stomach come and look. First, though, we'd better call the
sheriff and tell him."

She began to believe me. I could see the gray eyes

taking on a look of horror and comprehension. Without another word she went to a telephone that was on the kitchen wall. She raised the receiver and cranked. In a moment she said, "Get me the sheriff, Maudie."

Saarkinnen must have been sitting on his telephone, the answer was so prompt. Eve Vinson spoke coolly and calmly to him. "Sarky, this is Eve Vinson. There's some trouble out here. Mr. Hallam, you remember him, reports a dead man in his house." She listened a minute and turned to me. "Was it accident or—?"

"Murder," I said bluntly. "He was brained."

The hand on the receiver shook a little, but she relayed the information as I had given it, said, "Do hurry, Sarky," and hung up. Then she disappeared, returning with a coat over her shoulders and a scarf on her head. We went outside.

She was silent all the way to the house. Once there I stopped her at the door. "Maybe it isn't right to ask you to look at this, Miss Vinson."

She smiled that soft smile I liked so well. "I think I can stand it," she said. She pushed the door open and walked in. I stayed close behind, ready to catch her. But all she did was stiffen up, take two steps forward and say, "Oh! Good Lord!"

"You know him?"

Her face, when she looked at me, was white and the redness of her lips was like blood. She shook her head. "No. I never saw him before. But I know who he is.

"Mr. Prigwell. Joseph Prigwell!"

VI.

I could take just so much and I'd had enough for one evening. I found my way to the couch and flopped onto it. I started down at the corpse, and he was still a horrible sight.

"Miss Vinson!" I began. That was going to be too much to say if our relationship lasted as long as I liked to hope. So I changed it to, "Eve, this afternoon you told me you had never heard of a Mr. Prigwell. Now you say you never saw this man before but that he is Joseph Prigwell."

Her smile was, I thought, a bit on the pitying side, as if she were fully aware of my mental deficiencies and would be glad to humor me. She crossed around the corpse and sat down on the couch beside me. I gave her a cigarette and held a match for her, and finally she spoke.

"It's easily explained."

I grunted. I had heard that so often. I was willing to believe it, eager to believe it because I thought Eve Vinson an extremely swell girl and I found myself with a yen for her, but that wouldn't be the way the police would look at it. "Make it good for the cops," I counselled her.

"I saw his picture," she said. "In that envelope full of papers Mr. Burnham's chauffeur gave me this afternoon. At least it looked a lot like this man. Clothes and all."

That was better than I had hoped. At least she didn't try—as so many did when up against it—to convince the police she had seen it all in a dream or had a visitation. I said, "If you can stand it, take a close look at him. He's been dead a very short while, certainly not long enough for his estate to have been through the courts, so you could be the recipient of part of it."

"I've been thinking about that," she admitted, "since we came in here. I suppose Mr. Burnham can explain all that."

"He'll have to whether he wants to or not," I said, thinking of the big sheriff coming from Letsburg. Saarkinnen gave me the impression of being a man who would go after Burnham, Cadillac or not, and get some kind of answer from him.

"So," she smiled, "we can let Sarky worry about it for now. I want to see those clothes you told me about."

I took her into the bedroom. I showed her the closet. "Probably Prigwell's," I said, pointing to the overcoat and hat.

"The dresses aren't," she said. She fingered them. "They're new and very expensive." She went to the dresser drawers and looked at the lingerie. "And those are too. Everything is new." Her voice sounded a little wistful.

"But these?" I said. I held up the hose. She nodded.

"I think they're about my size too." She tried to smile. But I could see that she was closer to being frightened than she had been by the body in the other room. Probably for the same reason that I felt! The other could be coped with. It was reality. This had the flavor of fantasy, and not pleasant fantasy at that. She did manage the smile finally. "My size," she said again.

"Maybe I got drunk," I said, "and bought them with the idea of luring you in here. Only I don't drink that much." I was feeling sour. The reaction from all of this was setting in and it was a bad taste in my mouth. The peace and quiet of a small town! Blooey.

"These things," Eve said, "are lovely enough to lure almost any woman." Her eyes grew round and she jerked her head at me. "Mr. Hallam, Sarky might think—" She laughed a little, without heartiness. "It never occurred to me until now, but you know you are a stranger here. Sarky is very thorough and I'm afraid you're in for a stiff investigation."

"I can stand it," I said. "Only I won't like it, naturally."

"He did have you in his office this evening though," she hinted.

I let it go. I said, "You can't give me any idea on those clothes?"

"Nothing except that they came from a store that handles extremely expensive and exclusive lingerie. Spokane, perhaps, Seattle or Portland, or even from the East. Certainly not from any town near here."

I led her back into the living room. It was a grimmer place than the bedroom, but at least there was not the air of impossibility in that room. I went to my cupboard. "I have a half case of beer here, less one bottle I drank. We may as well try to drink the others. Or do you drink beer?"

"I studied journalism at college," she said by way of answer. "I'm expert at drinking from the bottle."

So I gave it to her that way. We sat on the couch, drinking the warm beer and looking alternately at Prigwell and at each other. I got up and put more wood on the fire. The room was at a pleasant temperature now; I hoped Saarkinnen would appreciate that. When I came back to the couch I brought two more bottles.

Eve accepted, tipped and drank. Then she said, "Mr. Hallam, are you sure you're innocent in all of this?"

"Hell, yes! The man is one I never saw before. I never heard of this town or of Letsburg until I stumbled onto them."

"Then I want to call you Tom," she said.

I set my bottle down and fussed with my pipe. "And if I'm a murderer you can't."

"Well, hardly," she answered. She looked quite serious. "Our acquaintanceship would be so short if you were. Sarky would be sure to catch you." Her gray eyes were awfully big looking into my face, and I'd had just enough beer so that her red lips were large and in focus while the rest of her face was a blurred white background. It was fascinating just to watch the movements of those lips.

"It wouldn't do to have too intimate a relationship with a man who was likely to be hauled off to prison."

"How intimate is using first names?" I liked the sound of all this, even though it made little sense at the moment.

"It leads to bigger things," she said, and hiccoughed gently. On two bottles of beer! I saw where I would have to get more, lots more, no matter what means I used. Malt beverages act that way on some people.

Before I could say more, or do more, on the subject, the damnedest noise I had ever imagined came from outside. First there was a scream that sounded like a siren keening close up and then a loud explosion; a short moment later a ripping crash came through the frosty air.

We both made our feet and the door at the same time. I decided not to stand on ceremony. I jerked the door open and went out onto the porch. The snow had stopped, a fine fat moon had slipped up over the top of the hotel, and the ground was dazzling white. Moonlight on the snow was beautiful, but I praised it not for its aesthetic effect right then but for the fact that it was almost as good as daylight. It took me about a minute to see what had happened.

From the hotel the old man was limping toward us. No one else was in sight. But the cause of the noise was obvious. From the spot where the pathway forked a plume of smoke was rising into the still, icy air.

Someone had blown the privy over.

Eve was standing beside me. She saw too. She began to giggle, hysterically, I thought. Finally she gave a gasp and subsided. "But—but," she pointed, "who was in it?"

Her Rabelaisian humor failed to strike me. I was placing the sound we had heard with the effect and I was sprinting for the overturned outhouse. Eve wasn't far behind, still laughing.

I stopped the scene. The smoke was still rising, but wispily and slowly now. The little house lay on one side, nails that had been ripped from its foundation timbers gleaming in the moonlight. Old Adam reached us and glared at me.

"I didn't do it," I said resentfully.

Eve giggled. I turned to her. "It isn't really funny. That bomb was a fake. I've heard them before." It was one of those Fourth-of-July affairs that they set off at public demonstrations. They scream as they go up and then explode and a flag billows out with a parachute on it and is floated to earth. Great stuff. Only this one had no flag, and the bomb had been aimed at the privy. "That outhouse was tipped over—probably by a crowbar," I said. "Look at the boards, not even scorched."

"But why?" Eve turned from me to Adam. He stood there, scowling, otherwise expressionless. "What would anyone go to all of that trouble for—just to tip over a privy?"

"This is not Hallowe'en," Adam said in a toneless voice.

A big bulk appeared from the porch and came toward us. It finally materialized into a massive figure of a woman. She was an incongruity. Her face showed traces of great beauty. Her eyes even now were luminous and dark and finely sized and spaced in her face. Her skin was still smooth and white and her hair was jet black, worn tightly drawn into a knot at the back of her head. Had she been thin she could have passed for less than forty, though she must have been fifteen years beyond it. But she wasn't thin. She was monstrous! She had to weigh three hundred pounds, at least. She swallowed the night and the surroundings and all of us with her immensity. She was obscenely fat.

This was Bossy. I knew it. Eve introduced her to me that way. "Adam's wife, Bossy."

"Well," she said, and her voice was thin and reedy. It startled me and I must have jumped, for she looked hard at me. "Well, what do we do? Set it up, Adam. Set it up, or the man will have to run into the house all night long." There was thinness in the voice but no lack of authority.

She was well named.

"Wait," I said. "We'd better leave this for Mr. Saarkinnen to see."

Eve stepped into the sudden silence. "We called him," she said, talking to the woman. "There's been some trouble. A man was murdered in Mr. Hallam's place this evening."

Bossy looked me up and down with those fine eyes so nearly hidden in fat. "City people! Trouble! All right, leave it. Adam, come inside. It's almost down to zero."

It was cold. I found myself becoming aware of the chill now that motion and excitement had abated. I looked at Eve. She hadn't yet taken off her coat but she was shivering. I was in my suit coat, little enough protection.

"You get in too, Eve. Both of you," she said. "If Saarkinen is coming he'll want food and coffee. Where do you want it?"

Eve evidently understood all of this. She said, "In our kitchen, Bossy. And he'll have two men with him. Coffee for—" she hesitated and counted a mentally pictured group—"seven. And get out the fruit cake. He likes it and it will save trouble." She shivered and turned back toward my little house.

I had no objections. If she preferred my company and that of a corpse while awaiting the sheriff, who was I to kick? It occurred to me that she might be wanting to keep an eye on me, but I brushed that aside. Charmer Hallam, that was the answer.

I was meditating on this, letting my puzzlement at the freakish practical joke slip to one side, when I heard the noise. It wasn't like the first one; this was easily recognizable. But it set me moving as fast.

It was the sound of a motor gunning, a deep, sweet sound as of a good big motor. And then the wail of tires fighting for a foothold on ice. It came from back, behind the carriage shed. I went that way with Eve after me. But I had a head start and I reached the shadows by the woodpile before she got started.

I went through the shadowy patch without slowing. My feet made speaking sounds on the frozen crust of the snow. I felt myself break through in the patches where it had drifted up a little and felt it slip inside my shoes. But I didn't stop. I thought "pneumonia," and kept on going because I had an idea of what had happened. And if I was right and whoever it was got away with it, both Eve and I would be in one hell of a spot when Sarky came up. Particulary Thomas Hallam.

I think I saw the car. I can't be sure because at the instant I rounded the shed and had a look at the road where this motor was spinning the wheels against the ice something hit me in the face. I heard the good sound wheels make when they find traction and start moving, and at that moment a blast of snow was thrown into my eyes and opened mouth.

I clawed and kept running, and someone stuck out a leg, and I tripped and went head first into the icy road. All I had for my pains was a mass of dirty ice and mud spun up by wheels thrown over me. The fall had knocked out my wind.

I came up gasping; Eve was kneeling down wiping at my face with the hem of her coat and making clucking sounds in my ears. The sounds were hardly the most accepted form of sympathy but they were soothing.

"The bastards!" she muttered. "The lousy bums. That was a hell of a trick, Tom. Tom?"

"Yeah," I said. I sat up and sucked in the night air.

"Did you see it—the car?"

"No," she said. "I heard it, so I could tell it again. I can tell makes of cars by their motors. It's a trick I learned when I was a kid. You know once at college—"

This, I decided, was no time for reminiscences. I said, "Damn it, did you see anything?"

She got sore; I guess I sounded rough. She dropped her coat from my face and scrambled to her feet. "All I did was hear it! I got here in time to see you clawing the road like—like a drunken porpoise!" And she turned and stalked off.

I got to my feet and went after her. "Sorry," I said. "Okay. I'm sorry. Only it wasn't any fun." I was limping and cold and my teeth were chattering.

She smiled at me, tilting her face up in the moonlight so that I almost forgot how miserable I was. "You aren't a porpoise really," she said. "Now you go in. I have to get something." She headed at double time for the hotel. I went into the house, bitterly reflecting that the peace and quiet of a small town—of this small town—were not what the doctor had ordered, exactly.

The warm air felt good. I headed for the stove, intending to stoke it so that the room would be good and hot. And then I stopped. It came back to me why I had run so desperately at the sound of the car and why the privy had been blown over with all that fake sound effect . I looked at the floor.

Mr. Prigwell had gone.

VII.

Now that, I thought, was swell. Mr. Prigwell disappeared. I am in the house alone. Eve has to take this time to go into the hotel. If she had furnished this cabin with a john she wouldn't have to go to the hotel, my mind reminded me, and then Saarkinnen wouldn't be wondering if I moved the body. Probably he would figure it was one of those things city people did on their off nights.

I went into the bedroom. I looked into the closet. There was nothing there but my stuff. I turned to the dresser and jerked open all the drawers. I saw my shirt, my pajamas, my underwear. Not in the right drawers, but put where they had been when the other stuff was added. Only that other stuff was gone now. All gone but the hose. They were crumpled in the bottom drawer.

"Probably," I said aloud, "the local ghosts won't stoop to hose with runners in them."

I heard the sound of the door opening and I went back into the living room. Eve came in. She carried a bottle. It was a big bottle, unopened. It was bourbon.

"I misjudged you," I said. I took the bottle tenderly from her hands. "Only it doesn't change things much. Notice anything missing?"

"Prigwell!"

I was satisfied; she had reacted. Very well. I didn't think it was a fake. Her eyes had gone huge and the color had drained so out of her face that the slash of red across her lips stood out like a livid scar.

"That's why all the fuss with the privy. The noise to get us outside and the privy to keep us gawking while this place was cleaned out. The clothes are gone, too."

"And the blood wiped up," she added. She took the

bottle away from me. She was much calmer than I was. She opened it, drew the cork, and went to my cupboard for a glass.

She poured a water tumbler half full of whiskey for me, made a small drink for herself with water and whiskey. She said, "Drink this down, fast. You'll have pneumonia with those lungs of yours."

I downed it. She built up the fire and then herded me onto the couch. Then she got a blanket off the bed in the bedroom, made me stretch out, and tucked me in. She said, "I'll get you another drink, only weaker than this. While I'm doing it you peel those clothes off. I'll bring dry things."

Since my "dry things" consisted of summer slacks or pajamas, I got pajamas. But she allowed me to wear underwear under them and belt my bathrobe on. A muffler, dry socks, and my fleece-lined slippers completed the costume. I felt like a fool writhing and wriggling and contorting myself under that blanket all because she wouldn't let me go into the chilly bedroom to change.

"And undo all my work?" she demanded indignantly. "I like you. I want you to stay alive—for a little while anyway."

"That's awfully nice of you," I mumbled bitterly through a mouthful of blanket. "I appreciate it tremendously. And I'll bet I've got everything on backward but my muffler."

"Next time you make an ass of yourself in the snow, let me know in advance and we'll get married," she said encouragingly. She smiled sweetly and passed me the drink. "Then we won't have to observe these little niceties."

I regarded her with a touch of fright. All these sympathetic touches. Tucking me in, being so solicitous. My God, had I found murder plus a designing woman? A horrible thought. No, hardly. I couldn't believe Eve was cooped up here away from men except by choice. Still, I had ducked such subjects as marriage for thirty years

and I didn't want to succumb in Vinson, Washington, at
eleven p.m. of a frosty January night.

She didn't look at all designing as she sat on the edge
of the couch and lit a cigarette, having rescued the pack
from my pocket. She was a damned pretty woman in her
odd way. "You'll probably be here for some time. At least,
Sarky will try to keep you here." She smiled softly but
there was meaning in the smile now. She drank and set
her glass on the floor. "Of course without gas or money
you couldn't go very far anyway, could you?"

"What have you been doing—checking through my
pants?"

"You dropped your wallet when you ran after that
car," she said. "I picked it up. I couldn't help looking.
After all, with murder and everything!" Her smile stayed
on. "I can use help on the paper if you want to stay."

I took a try at the bourbon and water. Maybe she was
a designing female. Maybe being married wouldn't be so
bad. I finished the glass, not saying anything. She took it
from my hands and set it on the floor, carefully, by hers. I
reached up and put my hand on her neck and pulled
gently. She twisted away long enough to set her cigarette
in the ashstand; then those lovely, large red lips found
their way to mine.

"We're drunk," I thought. "On beer, bourbon, and
excitement." I gave up rationalizing; this was no time for
it. ...

After a moment she stirred. "I wonder where Sarky is,
and poor Mr. Prigwell."

Romance, I thought! I murmured a little myself, "The
hell with them."

It was about five minutes afterward that the footsteps
sounded on the porch. Nowhere in the world do footsteps
as a class sound so much the same as those of the
American police. I sat up. "Saarkinnen!"

Eve's smile was dizzy and a little sideways, like a
slipped halo. "Think it over," she murmured.

Think it over? I watched her get up and go to the door,

swaying slightly. The sway certainly didn't detract from the nice movements of her figure. What was there to think over? Freud intruded; I pushed him aside. "This is love, after all those years," I chided myself.

Eve opened the door. Saarkinnen poured himself into the room. He looked at me. "Is that the body?" he asked without smiling.

I looked at Eve. "Am I a corpse?"

She dazzled the sheriff with that smile. "He isn't really; he's very much alive."

Saarkinnen snorted and turned abruptly as two men pushed their way into the room. "Shut the door ... So? Where is the body?" The last was addressed to me. But it took me a moment to get it, as I was savoring Eve's words. Nice feeling to know that a couple of years in a sanitarium hasn't taken away your technique.

I brought myself back to less cheerful subjects. "The body?" I said. "It's gone." I shut up and gave the conversational ball to Eve with a sort of mental reverse.

She stepped into the breach neatly. She evidently knew the sheriff well enough to realize that my inanity might cause a serious explosion. She was a little tight but she had enough wits about her to know what to do. She stepped forward, put one hand on Saarkinnen's arm, and looked up at him.

"It was stolen from us, honestly, Sarky."

I had an idea that those strange, lovely eyes of hers would have melted a harder character than Saarkinnen. The two men behind him looked from Eve to me.

"Yeah?"

"Yeah?"

Boy, I thought, this is going to be fine. Two intelligent under-officers to help the sheriff. But at least their words seemed to recall them to Saarkinnen's notice. "Might as well get acquainted," he said to no one in particular. "This is Mr. Thomas Hallam, boys. Mr. Hallam, you're liable to be seeing plenty of these men from now on. Barton and Martin. They're twins." He sounded a little proud, as if not every sheriff had twin deputies.

I wondered how he could stand it. They were as alike as the proverbial peas in the pod. Short and dark and squat, with curly black hair that grew low on their foreheads. Their faces, though, were the pleasant open kind a man is likely to get from associating too much with contented cattle. And their brown eyes had the same soft look. I don't mean they were complete drips; they just looked like it. Nor did it help matters that their rather nasal voices sounded exactly alike to an unaccustomed ear.

I acknowledged the introduction with a nod. It annoyed me that Saarkinnen had so obviously ignored our statement regarding the missing corpse. Evidently he refused to believe us.

He turned to his deputies.

"Bart, you go and see if Bossy's made anything for us to eat. Mart, get the flashlight out of the car and see what the privy looks like. Seems to me it was lying on its side when we came by."

"It was," Mart said. It must have been Mart. The other one was already out the door. When both were gone Saarkinnen pulled a kitchen chair to him, faced the back to me, and straddled the seat.

"Now, Hallam," he said, "let's hear your story."

I told it. When I got to the part about the slush in my face, Eve jumped up. "Sarky, I know about that car. I told Mr. Hallam but he didn't believe me."

Had she told me?

Saarkinnen just grunted at her. She said, "It was that Cadillac that was in front of the newspaper building today. The Mr. Burnham Cadillac."

"You sure?"

That got under her skin. "Have I ever been wrong on a car yet?" She looked triumphantly at me. "I can tell them by the motor sounds. I have funny ears."

"They're pretty," I said, currying a little favor with godfather. "And, evidently, clever."

Saarkinnen rose and spit into the stove. "Good ears," he admitted. "I never saw their like. Now, honey, you keep those ears open for Bart's old Model T."

Eve looked perplexed. "Bart's T?"

"Yeah. Mr. Hallam's friend, Burnham-Prigwell, got out of jail, swiped it, and took off tonight." He looked at me. "In plenty of time to get over here and help Hallam move that body."

VIII.

Bart or Mart, I couldn't tell which one, came in to inform us that Bossy had coffee and food in the hotel kitchen. "And," he said nasally, "she says you better hurry up or you don't get nothin'."

"She means it," Saarkinen said to no one in particular.

I got up and went with them, my overcoat draped over my bathrobe and pajamas. The procession started with Bart, then me, and then Saarkinnen sort of half holding Eve. "See that you don't slip, honey—" was the way he put it.

Mart or Bart, whichever wasn't the one leading us, detached himself from his examination of the privy and joined us as we reached the fork in the path.

"Nothin', Sarky," he said. "I don't see nothin'. An it's too damned cold out here anyway." It was Mart—I remembered that Saarkinnen had detailed him to the privy.

"Awful cold," Bart said from the front of the line. "Goin' below zero after the snow."

"Way below," Mart agreed.

Saarkinnen spat, quid and all, onto the nice white snow. "So?" he said disgustedly. "It's cold. Did you see any marks like of a crowbar maybe?"

"Yeah, on the foundation."

"Did you see where the bomb was planted?"

"Yeah, on the side away from the hotel. Dug a little hole along the foundation."

"Did you see anything else?"

"Yeah, footprints in the snow, only I stepped in 'em. They ain't much good now."

Jeez-us! I thought. Deputies! I said, "Any idea of what

kind of footprints they were?"

"Two kinds, little an' big."

"Like a man and woman?" Saarkinnen asked. "Like maybe, Eve and Hallam here?"

"About," Mart agreed.

"Sure," I said, "we were all around it after it was tipped over."

We let it go and trooped onto the back porch and started for the kitchen. Bossy appeared, or loomed rather, effectively blocking the doorway to warmth. But she couldn't keep out the tantalizing smell of fresh coffee and what I guessed were hot cakes.

"Get the snow off your dirty feet," she said. "My floor's clean. Keep it that way! Sheriff, get rid of your chew."

"Already did, back a ways, Bossy," he said mildly.

There was a great stamping of feet but it didn't fool Bossy. She stood outside the door and inspected us as we marched past her, single file. She turned Saarkinnen away.

"Go do a better job," she said in that pipe of a voice. And he turned decidedly away and stamped some more. I enjoyed it immensely.

But I wasn't to get off so easily. She came right up to me when we were in the kitchen. I don't mind admitting that I felt the cold and I was as close to the stove as I could get.

"Eve tells me you're liable to get pneumonia." Bossy looked up at me from those amazing eyes. "I've got something to fix you up." As if by magic she produced a jar of salve and a bottle of nasty, greenish-looking liquid from her apron pockets. "Rub this on your chest," she said, shoving the salve at me. "Keep it on, keep flannel over it. Keep warm. Here," she thrust the other forward, "drink this. Tonight, three times tomorrow. Indian remedies."

I dislike medicine intensely. I started to protest but from the side of my eye I saw Eve nod her head quickly. I just kept still, standing stupidly. It was Saarkinen's turn to laugh now.

"You'll do it, too," he said. "No cheating."

"He'll do it," Bossy said, in a tone that made me sure I would. "There won't be any sick people staying here." She moved so that she was looking at Eve. If she had been a small woman she would have swivelled; as it was she sort of flopped around. "He'll be healthy or you won't have him."

Nice, I thought; it seemed to be a conspiracy to shove her off onto me.

Eve smiled wanly at me, but said nothing.

Adam hobbled into the room just then and we all settled into chairs around the big kitchen table. Bossy lived up to her name and seated us. The table was round, so there was no head, but at the point nearest the stove she placed herself. Going around to the right were Adam, Bart, Mart, or maybe it was the other way around, Saarkinnen, myself, and Eve. Bossy had a good spot; she could reach out a huge arm and corral the coffee pot and the fresh, sweet cakes, and without turning she could watch Eve and me.

"No shop talk until the cakes are eaten," she said.

We stuffed ourselves. I was a little surprised that she was doing so when I was supposedly so near the grave, but she seemed to think they were good for me. She urged them onto us with her own particular idea of hospitality. She would thrust the cake plate forward and fix her victim with a determined eye. "Take one!" Victim is hardly the word, since the cakes were really delicious. Very thin and crisp and quite sweet. She had baked them fresh for us. They were, I discovered, Swedish.

I could hardly imagine myself in the center of a murder investigation. Here I was, the chief suspect from what I could gather, eating convivially with the sheriff and his deputies and the remaining secondary suspects. I had no doubt that the murderer would have been entertained as well had he been present and his status known.

I came to learn that people in this part of the country were like that. Formality was only a word to them, and a seldom used one. They bumbled through life without any class consciousness and seemed to thrive on it.

Saarkinnen illustrated the point neatly by telling a story.

"That Burnham-Prigwell fellow's a damned Easterner," he informed us.

"His accent did sound more or less that way," I agreed.

"Wasn't his accent," Saarkinnen disputed. "He had no manners. I was in a hurry so I stuck him in the cell with Indian Ike and old Pop Gormley right after Morozzi left. Pop's the town drunk," he added for my benefit. "Indian Ike's not so bad. He stinks a little sometimes, but that's because he doesn't like water. Never did like it, even as a boy."

"Anyway, this snooty Burnham-Prigwell starts yelling that he won't be put in the same cell with an Indian and an old drunk. I'll be damned!" Saarkinnen regarded us, one after the other, with his pale, washed eyes. "What's so bad about an Indian or an old man? Hell, we deloused them, didn't we?"

"Right off," Bart, or Mart, said.

"Before we put 'em in the bullpen," the other one affirmed. "They was clean."

"So," Saarkinnen explained, "Nutsy, the jailer, moved this Burnham-Prigwell, he was raising such a howl. I should have done it myself, but I was busy." He reached for another cake. "Darned if he didn't wallop Nutsy and break for it. Got clean away, too, and left the door wide open. I was so busy I didn't even hear him."

"I was eatin' across the street," Bart or Mart said.

"Me too," the other one explained.

"Wasn't the fault of you boys," Saarkinnen said pacifically. "As it was Indian Ike had to come out of the bullpen and help old Nutsy on his feet again. He sort of dusted him off, saw he was all right, and then went back in his cell. Nutsy locked the door and then came and told me. But Ike's got a sort of honor. He didn't yell a bit until Burnham-Prigwell got clean away."

I had to agree that Ike had honor—of a sort.

We finished the cakes and were smoking, with the last drainings of the big coffee pot in our cups. Mart and Bart sucked on corncob pipes that gave off offensive odors, while the sheriff, in deference to Bossy's rule about no chewing in the house, lit a surprisingly mild-smelling stogie. Bossy didn't smoke, it seemed, and Adam couldn't. I gathered that from the hungry way in which he stared at the sheriffs cigar. That gave me an idea and I tucked it away for future use. It was nice to know the little details about your future family.

"Now," the sheriff said, "we'll ask some questions. Hallam, let's hear about you."

"What about me?" I asked cautiously.

Eve, who had been silent and subdued during the eating, let one hand slide under the table edge and gently, timidly touched the side of my leg. I glanced at her and she smiled faintly at me. "You're sweet," her lips said without making any sound. Then she turned to the sheriff. "I can tell you more about him than he'll admit," she said.

"So?"

She nodded. "He's Tom Hallam. He was a columnist on the *San Francisco Mail* when I was in college. He was awfully good. He wrote editorials too. Our journalism class used them as models."

That was news to me. I had received more squawks than bouquets when I worked on the *Mail*.

"About three years ago his name just disappeared from the paper, so I stopped taking it," Eve said. "That's all."

"They fire you off the paper?" Saarkinnen asked me.

"No," I said, "I had a touch of lung trouble. I spent two years in a sanitarium in the mountains. Then the doctor told me to stay in the open. So I started wandering."

"So? Got a girl in San Francisco?"

I didn't like the way he said it. I shook my head and said, "After making all the arrangements for the wedding next week, this is a fine time to ask."

"Just remembered something," he said half apologetically. He dug into a pocket and pulled out a small envelope. It was plain, the kind you can buy at any ten cent store. "This came for you at the office," he said. "I brought it along."

I took it curiously. It had a special delivery stamp on it, but the stamp wasn't cancelled. It was addressed by typewriter and read, "Mr. T. D. Hallam, c/o Sheriff Saarkinnen, Courthouse, Letsburg, Washington."

"I don't know anybody who would send anything to me ..." I began.

"It wasn't mailed," Saarkinnen pointed out. "A kid brought it in. Joe Tucket's boy from the feed store. He was in the hotel buying candy when this woman called him over. She gave him the letter. Said she'd decided not to mail it. Gave him a dime, too. He brought it right over to me."

"Woman?" I knew of no woman who knew me closer than San Francisco.

Eve was staring at me with a puzzled, curious expression. Not so Bossy. She was definitely hostile. Adam seemed uninterested, as did Bart and Mart, who were chasing crumbs over the tablecloth.

"What did she look like?" I asked. I was feeling the back of the envelope with my finger. I would have bet ten of my dollars it had been steamed open.

"Boy didn't say. I asked him, but he claimed it was dark and he couldn't see her very well. Said she smelled nice and maybe she was light-haired and tall, and her voice was pretty. He's only eight."

I let the apology for Joe Tucket of the feed store's progeny hang in the air and opened the letter. There was nothing else to do. The eyes fixed on me demanded it. I had a good idea who had sent it, but I tried to give no sign of that. Besides, I was as curious to see what was in it.

There was a single sheet of paper, typed double-spaced. Even the signature was typed. That didn't bother me much. But the contents did. I felt like a man who has been thoroughly kicked in the midriff.

I read,

> *"Darling, I am at the Letsburg Hotel. Please don't*
> *avoid me any longer. It will be better for us if you*
> *see me right away and we get things straightened up.*
> *I will be here until you come. Your loving wife,*
> *Anitra."*

My loving wife Anitra! I handed the letter to Eve and reached for my coffee cup.

IX.

It was one of those things that break up the most congenial of parties. It certainly dispersed ours. Eve led the parade by standing up, not looking at me, and saying to the sheriff, "I think I'll go to bed, Sarky. If anything important comes up don't hesitate to wake me." Which meant that when he was through with me she would be available to him.

Bossy was more direct. She just glared at me and sniffed. Adam leaned across the table, thrusting his scowling face at me. "Casanova!" he hissed. If my position had been less precarious the whole situation would have been funny as hell. As it was, I felt like a tightrope walker who discovers, in the middle of his act, that some bright soul has let the wire go slack. And, too, I was hurt by Eve's attitude. The least she could have done, I reflected gloomily, was to trust her once potential husband. I took no particular pleasure in recalling that she had fixed herself onto me to be my wife, but nevertheless I hated to be misunderstood. Or so I told myself. When I had the time and thought it over I discovered I had quite a yearning for the lady.

Saarkinnen smiled blandly through the whole procedure, and when they had done having at me he got up, jerked his head at the door, and with me sandwiched between himself and his deputies, we filed back to my house.

We built up the fire and then I was seated in the easy chair facing the davenport on which the three of them arrayed themselves, Saarkinnen in the middle.

"All right, Hallam," he said, "let's get it over with. I don't know what your racket is but it isn't going to last long."

I spread my hands. "Hell, I—" I broke off and tried another tack. "How long have you been sheriff?"

"Twenty-five years," Mart or Bart spoke up.

"Since he got out of college," the other one said.

"Thanks," I grinned. Saarkinnen just looked at me. I said, "You've been sheriff a long time; evidently you're a good one."

"Good enough," he growled, "not to be soft-soaped."

"I'm not soft-soaping," I said, with just the right touch of anger in my voice; "I'm telling you something. A good sheriff is a man who uses his head. All right, use yours. If I have a racket, I'm sure a blundering idiot to lay myself wide open like you seem to think I have. If some woman who claims to be my wife were in on a racket with me, would she write me at the jail? Particularly a letter like that? And would I lay claim to a lot of stuff I can't prove about my background?

"I tell you I have no wife. I know no woman called Anitra, nor do I know the former owner of that corpse, or anything about the damned set-up. I'm willing to cooperate with you to find out what it's about, but I can't if you think I'm the big noise."

"It sounds good," Saarkinnen said. "So?"

"So," I said, "I'll tell you a story. I'm sure Eve would, if she hadn't forgotten it in all the excitement." That ought to help make me a gentleman; it sounded good. "This afternoon a big Cadillac was parked in front of her newspaper office. There was a fat man asleep in the back seat. When she and I got into the office a guy in a chauffeur's uniform was inside waiting for her. She didn't know him or the fat man, she said. But he gave her an envelope and skipped. The fat man was supposed to be Mr. Burnham, the executor of Joseph Prigwell's estate. The envelope she got contained papers and a two-thousand-dollar check as a part of Eve Vinson's share in that estate. She said she had never heard of Prigwell. She was telling the truth—that was obvious.

"Tonight when she came in here and saw the body she

turned pale as that snow outside. She said she'd never
seen the corpse in her life but that it was Joseph
PrigwelL"

Saarkinnen was stroking his chin with one big hand
and at the same time letting his jaw rise and fall on his
cigar stub. His pale eyes were watching me closely.
"Damned funny," he said. "And this man who got out of
my jail wasn't any one of those guys?"

"No," I said.

"You see anyone like this woman who says she's your
wife?"

"No," I said.

"Let's see that letter."

I handed it to him. He spread it on his knees and
leaned over studying it. Mart and Bart craned too. He
waved them back. "You can look at it later." He glanced
up at me. "Signature typed. Hotel stationery and I
suppose hotel typewriter. I can check on that. Maybe find
more about her."

"Paper like that carries good fingerprints," I said.

"Probably wore gloves if she's steering clear of the
police," he said. "But it's damned funny she'd send it to
the police station if she is."

I admitted it was. I said, "I'm not claiming Eve is in
this, sheriff. I don't think she is." I wasn't sure now, but it
wouldn't help my cause any to accuse one of the local
heroines. "But those papers she has might tell you
something. And that Cadillac—and the people in it. They
said they would be in Letsburg."

"Check up," he said. "Bart, take some notes."

The man on his left took a notebook and a stub pencil
out of his shirt pocket, wet the pencil, and began to write.
The sheriff seemed to be able to tell them apart. I wished
I could.

"Sheriff," I said, "let me help you on this."

"You might go see that woman like she asked," he
said. "Only how do I know you won't break for it?"

"Because," I said, "I'll leave my typewriter here and

you can have Eve lock the place up. No man who makes a
living writing will leave a typewriter unless he's
starving." For that to work he naturally had to assume I
was the writer I represented myself to be.

"All right," he said. I sighed with relief. So far it
seemed I was being trusted—to an extent.

"Only," he said, "don't feel too bad if it's your own
story you're writing, Hallam." He got to his feet. Bart and
Mart followed him. "See you in the morning," he said,
starting for the door.

That was more like it. I wished them all a cheerful
good night.

Saarkinnen turned and came up to me. "How many
sets of keys you got to your car?"

"One," I said, wondering.

"I'll take it," he told me. "And we'll come by for you in
the morning—save your gas."

I gave him the keys. Hell, yes, he trusted me!

X.

Saarkinnen arrived early the following morning, and we were soon on our way. There were chains on the car, and after a while the flip-flop of them on the pavement began to get on my nerves. I said cautiously, "Have any luck yet?"

He shrugged. "No corpse, no murder. Not legally, anyway. And no sign of this Cadillac you and Eve talked about. There's no Burnham registered at the hotel now."

"But there is someone there," I said. "And in a place the size of Letsburg all of the newcomers wouldn't be hard to spot."

"Two people," he said. "A man and his sister. I haven't seen either of them, but the clerk says he's young and nice-looking. Name of Roger Jocelyn. The girl is registered as Mrs. T. D. Hallam."

"And what does she look like?" As if I didn't know too well.

"The clerk says she's a blonde and tall. He can't remember much but her shape. Nice, very nice. Lots."

"That," I said bitterly, "is undoubtedly my loving wife, Anitra. Just how do I contact her, by the way?"

"Go into the hotel and sit. Ask around, maybe."

We passed through a long tunnel of forest. When a side road came whitely in on our left, Saarkinnen jabbed his finger at the trees. "That's where we got run in the ditch last night. Going to Vinson."

"You didn't look messed up," I said.

"We were coming along. It was still snowing. Mart was driving. All of a sudden a car without lights barreled out of that side road. Mart had to swing sharp to miss it.

We skidded and went into the ditch. It took us almost an hour to get out, or we would have been there sooner."

"What kind of a car?" I asked.

"Hell, we don't know. We didn't see anything but the shape of it coming at us."

"Think they meant to run you down?"

"No, I think they meant to put us in the ditch," Saarkinen said.

"And slow you up so they could knock the privy over and swipe the body," I suggested.

"So? Whoever it was is damned well smart enough to know what I'm doing," he answered.

"Anyone here or in Letsburg could have listened in on the line and found out, couldn't they?" I kept on.

"Yeah, or they could have been tipped off," he said.

"I didn't, if that's what you mean," I told him. I wanted to scotch any ideas he might have along that line before he got them started. "I was with Eve from the minute I phoned you—except when I went in and found the body gone."

"I thought of that," he said. "You know, Hallam, what interests me most about this case is that clothing you and Eve talked about." He rolled his window down and spit out the gnawed stub of his cigar. "That doesn't make sense."

"What does?" I asked. "A man dead a few minutes whose will was made and executed before he ever died? Or a punk like that chicken-burier having the names of both the dead man and the supposed executor of his estate? By the way, any news on Burnham-Prigwell?"

"None," he said. "Not a damned bit." He had a funny look on his face.

We wheeled into Letsburg then, swung off the main street and to the courthouse by the back way. Saarkinnen waved me away from the building. "Go on down to the hotel. I'll see you here when you get through."

I went around the courthouse square and onto the main street. It was still cold, with the snow scraped off the main street but piled in the gutters and on all the lawns I could see. A few stores were doing a half-hearted business. It didn't look much as if the war had fired Letsubrg to any enthusiasm, or any prosperity either.

I headed for the hotel. I went past one beer parlor and stopped. I was tempted to go in and get something to strengthen my resolve, until I remembered that no hard liquor was sold over bars in this state. I sighed and started on, glancing through the door.

What I saw brought me up right now. Inside, nursing a beer at the far corner of the bar, was a man who looked familiar. It was darkish and I had to take a second look before I was sure. But I couldn't mistake that sweater and cap. It was Burnham-Prigwell.

I went inside, slamming the door after me. He looked up as I charged for him. I yelled at the bartender, "Get that guy!" I was excited. If I'd gone in quietly or called Saarkinnen I might have had a chance. As it was, Burnham-Prigwell had all the time in the world to get away. He came straight at me, with the bartender scuttling down the bar in a haphazard fashion. Burnham-Prigwell threw the contents of his glass right in my face, went past me, stopped at the door long enough to get it open with one hand and heave the glass at the bartender with the other, and then he was gone.

"Call Saarkinnen," I sputtered. I was digging beer out of my eyes and cursing the day I had been spawned with such a weak skull. By the time I could see, the bartender was cranking his wall telephone.

"Here's the sheriff," he said.

"Saarkinnen," I yelled into the telephone. "Burnham-Prigwell is here." I told him what had happened. His slow chuckle came over the wire. He laughed at me!

"Quick thinker, isn't he?"

"You sure sound interested," I shouted back. "He'll be gone if you don't hurry."

"He'll be gone by now, anyway," Saarkinnen said with devastating logic. "But he can't get far unless he hitches a

ride. He can't do that without exposing himself. It's
too cold for him to stay out long. Don't stew."

I let it go. "All right," I said. "When I get washed up
I'll go over to the hotel." I slammed down the receiver and
asked for the washroom.

XI.

The hotel lobby was gloomy inside, with much the same kind of panelling as Eve Vinson's hotel boasted. But in this hotel there was at least some sign of life. Not much, but a little. The clerk behind the front desk was leaning rather somnambulantly on the counter, scratching his head with his fingertips and yawning over a ledger. He looked up without curiosity when I reached him.

"My name is Hallam," I said. "Is there a message for me?" That was the only way I could think of putting it. I would have felt like a fool asking for a wife I didn't possess.

"Hallam," he said. He went to the rack. "Initials?"

"T. D," I said. "Tom Hallam."

"Guess this is yours," he said. He handed me an envelope. It was hotel stationery, plain except for the name of the hotel in one corner and my name typed on the front.

I moved farther down the desk. Not far enough from where he worked to be out of the light but far enough to keep him from peering at my letters.

It was short and to the point, much like the message I had received via Saarkinnen. It read,

I am waiting for you. I am in room 212. "Please come so we can settle matters. Your wife, Anitra.

I jammed the letter in my pocket and looked around for the stairs. They were hidden off to one side of the lobby. I walked up to the second floor, along an uncarpeted hallway to where the numbers 212 were faintly outlined in peeling white on a dark door. I stopped and held my breath a moment, trying to hear something. But there was no sound. I shrugged. What else could I do? Even if I hadn't been curious to see "my wife," Saarkinnen was sufficiently on my tail to make this visit necessary. I knocked on the door.

There were perhaps thirty seconds' silence, then the sound of softly moving feet, a door being pulled shut quietly, and finally a woman's voice, husky and a little familiar.

"Who is it?"

"Your doting husband," I answered.

"Oh!" The door opened. I stared at Anitra. She was as beautiful and as hard as I remembered her. If I had chosen a wife for superficial appearance I couldn't have done much better. Instead of slacks she now wore sheer pajamas with a light robe thrown loosely over them. I had been correct on my first inspection. She was definitely built.

She led me inside. The room was clean and neat, but grubby, with a worn carpet on the floor and an iron bedstead in one corner. She sat in a deep chair with one leg over the edge. She was smoking a cigarette with quick, jerky movements.

She was hard, all right, and the veneer plastered over the hardness wasn't particularly thick. But figuratively she was a knockout. The pajamas were apple green and they showed off her hair. She knew she was put together and when she sat or walked or relaxed she did it with an eye to the effect on me. She succeeded in getting the effect; I wasn't any relation to a brass monkey after a cold spell.

She didn't say a word to me until I was seated on an aged davenport. Then she looked at me with a half-smile on her very red lips. "I suppose you're wondering—"

"That's right," I said. "Why pick me out to put on the spot? Or is it that your idea of gratitude for the lift I gave you?"

"You've been around enough to take care of yourself,"

she answered calmly. "And you're a stranger here, just as I am. In a burg like this strangers have to stick together."

"Or hang separately?"

She smiled, not pleasantly. "More or less, that's the idea."

I looked her up and down pointedly. "You look strong enough to wield a mean piece of stovewood."

She looked innocently at me. Her eyes were brown, a little too close together, and not very big. They expressed innocence about as well as her body did. "Why should I wield a piece of stovewood?"

"Who was Prigwell, by the way?" I asked.

"You aren't here to ask me questions," she said impatiently. Her smile had faded. "I'll do the asking."

"Where," she demanded suddenly, sitting up abruptly, "are my clothes?"

I knew damned well what she was talking about but I figured this might be just the place to play dumb. "As far as I know, you're wearing them," I said.

"I want those clothes and I want them fast," she said. "All of them."

"What clothes?" I looked as innocent as she had tried to.

I must have succeeded, because she jerked herself up and started striding across the room. That was the way she did it, taking huge, pounding steps. If she had had high heels on I would have matched her against myself for height.

"I'm going to the can," she announced. "Stay where you are." She opened a door and went through it.

Gentle soul, I thought, and reached for my pipe.

I heard no sound of running water but a moment later she came back. Her cigarette was gone, and she undulated toward me with her hands outstretched. She stroked my cheeks when she reached me and sat as close as she could without actually crawling into my lap.

"Darling," she cooed, "let's forget it. Let's start over. I was a fool before and I promise if you'll forgive me!" She sounded convincing, too convincing. A pair of tears glittered in her eyes. She kept her hands on my cheeks and pulled my head toward her. "Please, darling ..."

It was an embarrassing situation, at best. Either this woman had mental aberrations and really thought she was my wife or she was playing it so deep she was even trying to convince me that she was. And either way I was liable to get burned. I was beginning to sweat already.

She wasn't hard to look at. Her lips were more than tempting. Her eyes were saying anything but no. Besides, the grip she had on me gave me a hint that she might be stronger than I if it came to any actual struggling. I wasn't having any, but I didn't know how to go about telling her so.

"Wait a minute," I sputtered, sparring for time. "Let's get this straight."

She stopped mauling me but she didn't let go. "Get what straight, sweetheart?"

"This marriage business."

She let loose with one hand and tenderly stroked my forehead. "Poor Tom," she murmured. "Were those years they had to shut you up such awful ones?"

"It wasn't a bughouse," I told her. "I'm in my right mind."

"Amnesia," she said gently, softly. "Poor Tommy."

That was too much for me. Allure or no allure, I was getting out. To hell with Saarkinnen, I would rather risk my neck with him than with this woman. I bent backward, got out of reach of her hands, and twisted to my feet.

"I don't know what the hell this is all about," I said, "but take it to some other sucker. I've got proof of who I am—and it isn't your husband."

I started for the door, but she was quick. She got in front of it and stood there, her considerable chest stuck out at me. "Wait a minute," she said. Her voice was like the scrape of a chisel on a piece of rough rock. "You aren't getting away with it that easy." She put a hand on my chest and shoved. "Go sit down."

Since her push had landed me against the davenport and I slid onto the seat of it, all I had to do to comply with her request was to stay where I was. Right then I didn't feel much like arguing with her. It's an awful blow to a man's pride to let himself be pushed about by a mere woman, but mine was salved a little by reflecting on the size and general construction of her.

She went to the dresser, jerked open the top drawer, and without any rummaging pulled a rolled paper into the open. It was tied with a ribbon. She undid this, unrolled the paper, and then came up to me.

"Take a look," she ordered.

I looked. I reached too, but she held it away from me. "You aren't nearsighted," she said.

It was a marriage certificate. It announced to all who were interested that Anitra Mullen had been joined in holy wedlock to one Thomas D. Hallam four years before in San Francisco, California. It was neatly done, up to and including the scrollwork of angels on the borders.

"That's just fine," I managed to say. "But you've got the wrong Hallam."

She rolled the paper up again. "No I haven't," she said. Her voice was still hard and grating. "And what's more, I'm going to exercise my rights. I'm moving into your ducky little cottage and I'm staying there."

"Not with me," I said.

"With you," she said, coming down hard on the pronoun. "Until I get my clothes."

"I haven't got your clothes," I nearly yelled it. "And what if I were to take this fancy story of yours to the police?"

"Go ahead," she shrugged. "I still have our marriage certificate. And if I need it, darling, proof that you were locked up before for just this sort of loss of memory."

I snorted at that. "I can get witnesses to swear to my whereabouts since the day I was fool enough to be born."

"That would take time," she said smoothly. "My

witnesses are here already."

"Just what do you want?" I demanded.

"My clothes, darling, and you." She smiled sweetly. "You, of course, for a while anyway."

I felt myself trembling inside. I didn't like it. When I got that mad I wore myself out, and the doctor had told me to take it easy. But I couldn't seem to stop. I kept getting madder all the time I looked at her. It was the weirdest form of the badger game I had ever heard of. I didn't know how I had managed to become involved and I wanted to wash my hands of the whole affair. I wanted to live peacefully with Eve Vinson in the somnambulance of her hotel and newspaper, not run with a bunch of madmen as I seemed to be mixed up with.

She kept getting bigger and more beautiful and tougher as I looked at her. Her smile was a mocking one now, or so it seemed. She was just daring me to do anything about the spot she'd put me on. The trembling inside got so violent I began to sweat heavily. I turned and reached onto an end table as if I were going after a cigarette. I knew now what I was going to do. My hand closed around a glass ashtray. I got up very deliberately, measured my distance, and with the ashtray in my fist hit her full on the jaw.

I stepped over the spot where she landed and walked out the door, down the stairs, and right on to the street. I felt swell. When I reached the street, I realized I still held the ashtray. I turned and looked up at the hotel. I spotted the room I thought she must be in, pulled my arm back, and curved the ashtray right through the window.

XII.

I had no liking for the idea of going to see Saarkinnen, but neither did I want to walk back to Vinson. I moved down the street toward the beer parlor where I had spotted Burnham-Prigwell. So far no one had come from the hotel after me. I wondered if they were accustomed to having people heave ashtrays through their windows or were just too friendly to take issue with a stranger. I didn't much care. My mood was hardly a pleasant one. I was on a three-way spot, and I didn't like the situation. With Saarkinnen, with Eve, and with "my loving wife, Anitra."

I passed the beer parlor and deliberated on going in and getting as stinko as I could on beer. I turned toward the door—and pulled up short. This was becoming fantastic. For the second time that day I saw Burnham-Prigwell in there. Just as before, he was in the shadows at the far end of the bar nursing a glass of beer. The same bartender was behind the bar. He was perched on a stool, near the front windows, reading a magazine. Otherwise the place was deserted.

I began to think my mind was playing tricks on me, that I was having one of those peculiar sensations of memory in which it seems that the same thing has happened before in the same circumstances, and yet the whole thing is impossible.

At least this time I would make no fool of myself. I opened the door and went in quietly. The bartender raised his head, looked at me, and then went comfortably back to his reading. Burnham-Prigwell didn't move from his position. This time when I went toward him, he just looked at me.

I gathered that he and the bartender had reached an

agreement of some sort. Or, I wondered, had my interview with the tall, luscious, and tough Anitra affected my mind? Burnham-Prigwel nodded pleasantly at me. "Have a beer, fellow?"

"Not in the face this time," I said. "You have a hell of a nerve. Don't you know the sheriff's office is looking for you?" Or were they? Saarkinnen had impressed me as being hardly interested when I had called him the first time I had seen Burnham-Prigwell in there. Maybe it was a local custom to give a criminal the run of the town unless he went about making a nuisance of himself. I wouldn't doubt it.

Burnham-Prigwell chose to ignore my question. He grinned at me with thin lips. "What are you doing in Letsburg again?"

The bartender had raised himself sufficiently to draw me a beer. When he had returned to his magazine, I took my glass and sucked at the foam. To hell with it, I thought; if no one here was interested enough in an escaped criminal it was no skin off my nose. I wasn't going to worry over it if Burnham-Prigwell wouldn't.

"I'm in Letsburg," I told him, "because I can't get out. My car is in Vinson and I don't want to ask Saarkinnen for a ride home. So I sit here." I glowered at him and turned catty. "Or do you know a Model T I might borrow from someone?"

His smile was exasperatingly enigmatic. I still didn't care much for his looks. And for some reason the cultured voice that didn't fit his "dese and dose" appearance annoyed me. He still wore the turtle-neck sweater but his cap was stuffed into a pocket of his trousers. His hair was a nondescript brown, thinning on top. He looked a little better without the cap, but not much.

"Finish your beer and I'll drive you home," he said. "I've been planning to see you anyway."

I examined the suggestion while I drank. He didn't look particularly dangerous. On the other hand, he wasn't the pleasantest sort for a playmate. But what could I lose? Maybe he would drive me back to Vinson. Once there I could phone the sheriff. And maybe I could find a few minutes to try to explain things to Eve.

"I'm ready," I said, setting down my empty glass.

Burnham-Prigwell tossed a dime on the counter and reached for his cap. "Out back," he said.

We went that way, through a door and into a brick-paved alley. A decrepit Model T coupe was parked by the door. We got in. The self-starter ground the motor just enough to make it catch. We started off with a jerk that nearly threw my head through the windshield. Once we skidded as we swung out of the alley onto a sidestreet that finally led us to the highway.

"Sorry," he said as we kept jerking. "It's been a long time since I drove one of these."

"This belongs to Bart—Saarkinnen's deputy?" I decided that being subtle was a waste of time. To get an answer the best way was to ask.

"Nice of him, wasn't it?" he said amiably. He fished inside his sweater and brought out cigarettes. I refused and he lighted one for himself. We were driving right down the main street. When we passed the hotel he glanced at me.

"Have any luck in there?" he asked courteously.

I was about to ask him what the hell business it was of his, but I didn't. Evidently private matters were public in these parts. It was, I had to admit, no screwier than his being able to stay in plain view in a town the size of Letsburg, drive down the main street in a stolen car and get away with it. If he could do that, he must have something that entitled him to ask questions. I thought about it for a while, and what I decided made me glad I hadn't given him a nasty reply.

"I had no luck at all," I said.

We were on the highway now, jerking, bouncing past the rows of forest. It was almost noon, but the low-hung January sun wasn't doing much good and clouds were scuttling in on the breast of a south wind to obscure what little sunlight there was. I was getting cold.

"We're due for another snow," he said conversationally. "I wonder if Bart left chains somewhere in this jaloppy."

"You should have swiped Burnham's Cadillac instead of this heap," I said. I watched him for a reaction.

His head jerked around at me; then he swung back and looked at the road, "just how well acquainted are you with that Cad?" he asked. His voice wasn't the pleasantly conversational one of a few moments before, nor was it the tone he had used before Saarkinnen. It was a tone of authority such as I heard innumerable times during my early days of police reporting.

The voice and the way he had looked at me confirmed my suspicions of him. I said, "Who are you working for—Fatso Burnham?"

"Hardly," he said. "Hallam, you're on a spot, so I'm going to let you in on something. But I'm warning you, if it gets out to anyone—I mean anyone—I won't help you a damned bit. Right now I think you're an innocent victim of circumstances, but you can get in deep. And if you shoot off your face or try to hide behind my skirt,

I'll feed you to the wolves."

That was swell. Now I knew exactly where I stood. Was this guy as screwy as everyone else I had met lately? I just looked at him. There wasn't much to say and I was going to let him say it. He had made it plain that he wasn't my best pal, and if he would explain the rest of his gibberish as well I might learn something. I waited.

He dug into his sweater again and came up with a flat leather wallet. He nipped it open with his thumb and without taking his eyes off the road extended it to me.

I needed only one look to make a lot of things clear. I said, "Put it away," and he did. I got my pipe and lit it. There were a few flakes of tobacco in the bottom of the bowl, enough so I could get some smoke and make a noisy sucking sound.

I said, "All right, so you work for Uncle Sam instead of

Burnham. But why all the rigmarole? Why call yourself
Burnham and Prigwell? And why tell me I'm on the spot?
I'm not liable for income-tax evasion, God knows."

"That's not my worry," he said. "Let Morgenthau stew
about that. The Treasury Department is interested in
other things besides income tax."

"I suppose Saarkinnen knows."

He grunted. "I had to tell him. He was getting in my
hair. Every now and then you run into a small-town
sheriff who is smart enough to help. Sometimes they're
too smart and then you're stuck. A small town is a tough
place to hide yourself in."

"But why the act of busting out of jail?" I asked. "If
you hadn't done that, you wouldn't have the necessity of
hiding yourself."

"I was trying to save Prigwell's neck," he said. "But I
was too late. And that reminds me about that Cadillac ..."

"All I know," I said, "is that I saw it on the road and
then in front of Eve Vinson's newspaper office. It
contained Fatso Burnham. His chauffeur was inside the
office. A too pretty young fellow. And Miss Vinson claims
it was the car that drove out of the alley last night when
Prigwell's body was taken out of my place."

"I got most of the story from Saarkinnen," he said.
"Did you get a good look at Burnham?"

"All I saw," I told him, "was a Homburg hat and a fat
face buried in a fur coat.. Enough to make me think he's
probably a repulsive, overfed slug who made himself fat
at the expense of a lot of others."

He grinned. "That's snap judgment from a distance."

"Am I right or wrong?"

"I don't know," he said. "I've never been able to get
close enough to him to find out. I'd like to, though."

"What's he done?"

"I don't know that either," he said.

I let it go and tried another tack. "Do you know
anything about Anitra, my self-styled wife? The woman I
went to the hotel to see."

"A little," he admitted. "She's dynamite."

"I found that out," I said. "She's also screwy." At the risk of his thinking I was batty I told him.

"She got me in her room and then started insisting she was my wife and that she wanted her clothes."

"Oh!" he said. "By God, I thought that was it."

"What?"

"The clothes—go on."

"That's all," I said. "First she tried to convince me I was her husband by making passes at me—you've seen her?"

"Yeah," he said. "So you have an iron will and the passes failed."

"They failed," I admitted. Let him assume I had an iron will if he wanted to. "Then she got tough. She shoved me clear across the room and showed me our wedding certificate. My God, I knew I never married her. I've never been that drunk."

"A certificate, huh? Did she try to make you believe you were drunk when you married her?"

"No," I said, "she tried to make me believe I was crazy afterward, though. That I spent two years in a nut house."

"I though it was a t.b. sanitarium."

"So did I," I said. "And it was—I can prove it, damn it."

He sort of grinned. She wasn't trying to be his wife so it was funny to him. It could have been funny to me, I suppose, but it was more bewildering. I was the kind of guy who had had little to do with women and then in the space of less than twenty-four hour I'd found myself proposed to by one and more or less married to another, both of them perfect strangers.

My companion said, "After she proved you were married: then what?"

"Then she said she was going to move in with me until I produced her clothes."

"And what will you do with her?"

I shrugged. "I don't think she'll show up," I told him. "I got mad and belted her with a glass ashtray and walked out. Then I threw the ashtray through her window as a reminder. I think she'll leave me alone."

"I wouldn't count on it," he said. "She'll be after you with a vengeance now."

"Swell," I said. "And all I have to do to get out of it is produce some disappearing clothes."

"The ones that were in your place, you mean?"

"I suppose those are the ones," I said. "Hell, she'll have to find Prigwell's body snatcher—I think he took the damned clothes."

"No, I took them," my driver said. He looked sidewise at me. "They're Government evidence against you, Hallam," he said cheerfully.

We were bumping along on the last lap to Vinson now and the sky was totally obscured with thick grey clouds. They matched my mood. What the devil, I wondered, did he mean by the last crack?

It had seemed bad enough for a person who thought of himself as an innocent bystander, as I had, to become involved in murder, but to find the Government on his tail at the same time was almost too much.

I said, "That's fine and what have I done to the Government?"

The look he gave me was vaguely amused. "I don't know that you've done anything," he told me. "As I said, you look like an innocent victim of circumstances. But I'm just letting you know if you aren't innocent I have what it takes to put you in our private hotel."

I wasn't scared. I was disgusted. And slightly annoyed. I felt now much as I had just before I had lost my temper with Anitra. The only difference was that this annoyance wouldn't turn to violence. I didn't get mad that way very often. If I had, I would have been back in the sanitarium. It takes a lot of energy to get really angry.

But I was annoyed, so I wasn't as frightened as he wanted me to be and enough to do something about the situation I was in.

"Please, mister," I said cajolingly, "send me to Alcatraz so I'll be close to home." And I added a two-syllable word derived from the Anglo-Saxon.

He took time to light another cigarette. "You don't scare, do you, Hallam?"

"Sure," I said. "Show me a gun or let a guy bigger than me start swinging and I'll run like hell. But that's a damn sight different from having an educated cop try to tell me I'm due for a Federal rap because I happened to be in the same place with some mysterious clothes."

The glance he sent toward me was speculative. "Even when the clothes are contraband?"

"Are you working for the OPA?"

"No need to get sarcastic, Hallam," he admonished. "I'm working for the Customs. On the hunch that those clothes were smuggled across the line. It could tie in with the OPA, of course, since a black market is the best way to get rid of the stuff.

"But my interest is collecting duty, not worrying about price ceilings."

I had to laugh at that. "You wouldn't get to first base hanging something like that on me," I said. "I've never been near any border except the few times I went to Tiajuana in the old days."

"A man travelling," he said quietly, "with a good excuse to be deferred from the draft, has a swell chance to make contacts. He wouldn't have to cross the line and do the buying personally."

"What's your name?" I asked abruptly.

That caught him off stride. He blinked at me. "Dirkson," he said. "Why?"

"I'm tired of thinking of you as Burnham-PrigwelL" I said. "And I just wanted to know what to call you when I tell you off for being such a first-rate damned fool."

We stopped right there. Dirkson got out of the car and stretched his thin body.

"I want to take a look at your place, Hallam. Want to

give me a key?"

Which meant that he wanted to do it without my being there. I could have argued with him, refused him permission to search my belongings, or have been less stubborn and insisted on going with him, but there wasn't much point to it. My refusal would only have confirmed any suspicions that he might have of me, and he could accomplish his purpose by getting a search warrant from Saarkinnen. Besides, getting rid of him might give me a chance to see Eve alone, and I had things to say to her.

I said, "Go on in. There isn't any key. I am reliably informed that they don't use keys in this part of the country."

He grinned a little at my disgust and walked off. I swung around the other side of the carriage shed and went down the driveway toward the street.

XIII.

Eve was sitting under the shaded light, working at her desk. As the door closed she looked up.

"Hi," I said lamely, "any big stories today?"

I didn't know what to expect, a brick or a good cussing out. Or tears. But I got none of them. Her smile was definitely friendly. "Come on over," she said.

I went around the counter and up to the desk. She half rose from her chair, her face up expectantly. It was quite different from Anitra's technique. I didn't stop to analyze this time. Here was Eve's face; I kissed it. She got all the way out of her chair, wrapped her arms around my neck and returned my kiss. I mean with interest. We were both breathing quite hard when she wriggled loose and dropped on the edge of the desk.

"Got a cigarette, darling?" Her soft voice and lovely eyes would have melted a better man than I ever hope to be.

I gave her a cigarette and because I felt I deserved it, took one myself.

"I thought you were mad at me," she said naively, blowing out the match I was trying to hold. "I looked for you all morning."

I sat on the desk too. "Saarkinnen came in this morning and hauled me off to Letsburg to visit my wife."

She smiled and her peculiar beauty came up and hit me another jolt. But it went away under a sensation of relief. The smile meant everything was okay.

Eve bounced up and down like a little kid. "Tell me about your wife. Is she pretty?"

"Beautiful," I said. "Tall and well built—and as hard as nails."

"Did she make love to you?"

"She tried," I said.

"And what did you do?" Her eyes were round and wondering like a child engrossed in a fairy tale. All for effect, but it was flattering.

"I hit her on the chin and left," I said.

"You clipped her!"

"I should leave you after that pun," I retorted. "It was strictly a platonic punch."

The impish grin faded. "But what did she want?"

Here was the tough part. I was having a hard time believing myself that I wasn't married to Anitra. That certificate looked more genuine than any real one. How was I going to convince Eve it was a put-up job? That I had never seen Anitra before except to give her that lift, nor, as far as I knew, had she seen me. And all of that made her possession of a wedding certificate all the more in congruous—and the harder to explain away.

I put my cigarette out in an ashtray. "Look," I said, "I never saw the woman before." I decided not to say anything about picking her up on the road. "I never want to see her again—but I probably will. I don't know how she did it, but she has a marriage certificate with my name on it. It's four years old, comes from San Francisco, and looks genuine, even to my signature."

"Tom," Eve wailed, "you didn't, really—"

"Hell, no," I said gruffly. "Not even when I was drunk. I've never been married. I don't know how she did it or why, but it has me in a crack."

"That's impossible. How could she fake it?"

"When not even I was positive I was ending up here until I arrived," I finished for her. "Damn it, I know it sounds screwy, but there it is."

"But why?"

"All I know," I said, "is that those fancy underthings and dresses we found were hers. And she wants them back."

"And we haven't got them," Eve said. "What will she do?"

This was the part I particularly disliked telling her. "I'll tell you what she said," I told her. "Move in with me as my wife until I produce them."

Eve's lip curled. "What a charming character!"

"I wish," I said miserably, "you'd believe me. We're both in quite a jam—" I stopped! I couldn't tell her about Dirkson. Not after the warning he had given me.

"I'm trying to believe you, Tom," she said earnestly. "Awfully hard." She stopped and looked as if she were concentrating. "I'm in a jam, too?" she asked finally.

"Sooner or later your letter and legacy from Prigwell will come out and then you will be," I said.

"Oh, Sarky knows me; he'll believe me."

"I hope so," I said feebly. Sarky wasn't Dirkson—and Dirkson didn't know her. I didn't even know her; and I wasn't awfully sure just what connection there was between Eve and Prigwell.

She wasn't watching me. She seemed to have forgotten I was there. For a moment she stared at the brown linoleum floor, then, hopping agilely off the desk, she walked to the rear of the shop. She was almost obscured by the gloom there. All I could see was the whiteness of her skin in the dark. I watched her and waited. I thought maybe she was trying to get up courage to tell me about her connection with Prigwell.

If she loved me as she said she did and she was in trouble, it might take a bit of doing to get up nerve to tell me about it. I wondered if I shouldn't go and try to help her. I decided it was better to let her work it out for herself.

"Tom!"

"Yes, dear?" My God, I thought, I sound married already.

"I have an idea," she called to me. I went back to see, since she stayed where she was.

She was in the shadows by a case of type, and she held out her hands and when I took them she drew me to her. There was a purposeful note in her voice, but the way she cuddled against my chest was wholly feminine. She was a funny combination.

"Do you really love me, Tom?"

"Yes," I said as well as I could with a mouthful of hair.

"And you want to marry me?"

"Of course, sweet."

"And you aren't married—not the tiniest bit?"

I didn't know where this was leading me and she was far too close for me to care. "No," I said. "I've never before come close to getting married."

She stepped back. In the dimness I could see that her eyes were excited. "I believe you. And I have a wonderful idea. We can fool that old—that woman! Let's get married now. Right away. We'll drive north to a place I know."

"Grand," I said, "but how does that fool her?"

"Why, she'll have to prove her marriage then. Don't you see? If she makes her claim again after we come back you'll be arrested for bigamy. Then she'll have to put up or shut up. Isn't it wonderful?"

"Wonderful" I echoed. "How do we get there?"

"In my car," she said. It's only fifteen miles. Let's hurry, darling!"

XIV.

It wasn't as simple as she made it sound. But I could see the advantages. And she was right—if anything could take me off the spot I was on, this should do it.

Our first problem was getting to the car. Her car was in the opposite end of the carriage shed from mine and parked by the shed was the dilapidated Model T Dirkson was using.

We went quite quickly down the driveway and reached the carriage shed. Eve looked at the Model T. "That's Bart's," she said. "The one that was stolen last night. Maybe we'd better call Sarky, Tom."

Her hand was gripping my arm and she was peering excitedly as far as she could see.

"Let's get out of here," I said. "If we call Saarkinnen we'll never get married today. Anyway," I added with an attempt at facetiousness, "that may be Mart's car."

"That's right," she agreed. "I can't tell their cars apart, except when the motor is going. We don't want him to catch us."

She unlocked the door to the shed. "Hurry, Tom."

I went after her and crawled, slightly numb at the thought that Mart and Bart actually had similar cars, onto the seat of an ancient Moon roadster. The thing looked at least twenty years old, with its square-cut radiator and old, odd lines. But it had a slanting windshield and a French top, making it look like something belonging to a high-school boy.

Eve stepped on the starter and the car roared into violent life.

By the time we returned, properly wedded, it was evening. Eve kissed me brightly and suggested:

"We'll get Bossy to cook a wedding supper, darling. I

have some old wine stored away. We'll call Sarky and invite him—everybody. And then—well, where do you want to live? The hotel or the little house?"

"I like the little house," I said, "but you'd better keep most of your stuff in the hotel until I get straightened around and out of jail.

"Do you really think you'll go to jail, Tom?"

"Don't you? Saarkinnen isn't overly fond of me; besides, I pulled a runout on him today. I was supposed to report about my meeting with Anitra."

"Not tonight," Eve said gaily. "We'll fill Sarky up at the supper and he'll be too comfortable to arrest anyone."

We pulled into Vinson. It hardly seemed changed at all. With the difference in my own status so definite, I had half expected the place to look altered.

There was one thing, though. We saw it as we drove around the carriage shed. The Model T was gone. Parked in its place was the big Cadillac, and the corpulent Mr. Burnham was visible apparently asleep in the rear seat.

"A short marriage," I commented as I closed the garage doors on the rear view of the resting car.

Eve looked genuinely worried. "Do you think it's she?"

"I'm damned if I know what to think," I admitted truthfully. "This whole thing is a muddle to me. How they came to pick on me, on you, in the first place. But I'll bet she's connected with this outfit."

Eve didn't answer that. Instead, she turned and started walking slowly toward the hotel.

I caught up with her. "Look here, darling," I said, "if there's something troubling you—if I can help? Is it this Prigwell business?"

She shook her head. "There's nothing, Tom." She was silent.

That was that, so I gave it up. I felt quite convinced there was something and that I should be in on it, for her protection and my own. There was nothing to do but wait until she was ready to tell me or until Saarkinnen pried it out of her.

She stopped when the path had brought us to the fork. "You'd better go on into your house and see," she said.

"And you?"

"I'll go to the hotel and wait for you."

I tried to grin at her and made a pass at ruffling her hair. "That's a hell of a way for a bride to look. Get a smile on. Go spread the news to Bossy; phone Saarkinnen. Start the party rolling."

"With her in there?"

"If she is," I said with a blitheness I didn't feel "I'll get rid of her."

Eve smiled then, a typically feminine smile. "Invite her to the party. We'll see what happens." The idea seemed to lift the gloom from her, and with a wicked grin she ran on toward the rear of the hotel.

I went less cheerfully and more slowly toward my house. I tried to look in before I opened the door, but the shades were drawn. I listened for a minute or two but could hear no sound. "Fine," I thought, "maybe I'm due for a headache."

It was cold and I couldn't stand there in the snow forever. And I was getting mad inside. I held the trembling in as well as I could and opened the door.

With the shades down the room was gloomy. Only a dull light seeped in around the edges of the windows. For a moment I could make out only the familiar lumps that were the furnishings. But I noticed that the room was warm. Someone had built a fire.

Then I saw him. He was sitting easily on the couch, quite relaxed. There was a gun in his hand. Now, I don't like guns. I've never had much contact with them, just enough to find them repellent.

I pulled the cord that turned on the overhead light. It threw the man into harsh relief. It was Burnham's too handsome blond chauffeur.

"Sit down, Hallam."

I said, "Thanks. What the hell are you doing here?" I

was scared, so scared I didn't know whether the trembling mounting in side me was anger or fear. But I didn't want ro let him know it.

"Waiting for you," he said in a smooth, chatty voice.

I sat down in my little typing chair and looked at him. I hadn't liked his looks the other times I had seen him. This time I regarded them with positive aversion.

"What do you want?" Not that I didn't have a damn good idea.

"The clothes," he said. "And fast."

I started thinking. It was easy with that carelessly held gun resting on his knee. The sight of this ugly blackness stimulated my mind as nothing else could have. It was pretty obvious, I reasoned, that the parties involved thought I had the clothes. Why not keep them thinking that?

"How about a trade?" I asked.

His eyes weren't pleasant to look at, but by concentrating on staring above the gun I managed to hold his gaze.

"Shoot," he said.

"I want information," I said. "Lots of it. You want the clothes."

"And I've got the information?"

"I think so," I said.

"Go on."

"Prigwell," I said. "Where is he? Who is he? Who was he?"

"Go on."

"What's the idea of this so-called wife of mine? And how did you ever figure me in on this?"

"You take a lot for granted—assuming I know all these things," he said. His voice was flat; I could tell nothing from it.

I was getting impatient. He was playing coy. To hell with that; I hated to sit and wait for anything.

"To hell with you; if you don't want to talk, forget it— all of it." I waited for him to answer that one.

"The clothes," he said.

"Scare me," I bluffed. He had, and plenty. "I don't know any more than you do."

I don't know what he would have done then if we hadn't had the interruption. I doubt if he would have shot me. He thought I knew where the clothes were. For some reasons they were important. Hell, I didn't even know why he wanted them so badly. There were others where they came from. And as for their being evidence, according to Dirkson they were traceable to me.

But the interruption did come, in the form of a wailing siren. It keened into the room crystal clear through the cold outside air.

"Cops! You double-crossing son-of-a-bitch," he yelled at me. The suave young man was gone. I thought for a minute he would shoot me before he left. He stopped glaring at me suddenly and bolted for the door. For a man with a limp he made time. I made a grab for him, half out of instinct and partly because I wanted him as Exhibit A for Saarkinnen.

He slapped at me with the gun barrel, then let me have it with his foot. I took the kick in the stomach, said "oof" and sat down hard. The door slammed while I was still trying to get my breath.

I was a hell of a hero. All those I had read about would have taken a whole roomful of men, and I couldn't even handle one lone guy with a small gun.

I got my breath back and made it out of the door just in time to see the big Cadillac start down the driveway. I took a good look. The angle was bad, the air was full of snow, and the light was poor, but I was willing to swear it wasn't the chauffeur who was driving that car but Anitra. A woman, surely. I had seen a white face, and that unmistakable and strong profile.

I went back inside cursing the stupidity of police who always insisted on displaying their own importance with a wailing banshee of a siren.

I was hungry, so I opened a bottle of beer. Nursing it,

I prowled through the house. The chauffeur, I saw, hadn't spent his time idly. My stuff in the bedroom was piled all over the floor. The drawers were pulled out; the dresser stood away from the wall. Bedding was piled carelessly on the floor and the mattress lay askew.

I left things exactly as they were and started out of the room. The carpet had been lumped up when the dresser had been jerked from the wall. Gracefully my feet found the high spot and I nearly took a header.

I recovered myself and spilled only a little of the beer. I set the bottle down and went to the edge of the rug, intending to jerk it back into place. If I didn't, I knew I'd stumble on it whenever I got close to it.

Tugging didn't have much effect, since the dresser was on part of the rug and the bed on another. I got against the wall to the right of the door and started to roll the rug up. I planned to roll it as far as the foot of the bed, lift up the bed with my shoulder, and shove the roll of rug past it. If I did that, all the way to the opposite wall, I could get the thing against the baseboard where it belonged and then roll it smoothly back again. I had bunched rugs before and no other way I had ever tried had ever worked.

I had it rolled about halfway when I saw it. In the far corner, where the closet was. It was a trap door.

"A haunted house, no less!" I grunted. "Secret passages and all."

But I was disappointed. There was a ring in the floor that lifted the trap door. I pulled it and it came up easily. I went into the other room and got my weak but still serviceable flashlight from my desk drawer.

A flight of wooden steps led down into a room the size of the two upstairs. It was dirt-floored. The walls were lined with shelves. On them were mostly dusty, empty fruit jars. It was a storage cellar, no more.

I hadn't expected to find Monte Cristo, or even Prigwell, but I was not prepared for the lack of anything. I don't like cellars, so I hurried. It was too cold and damp for me there. And if I hadn't run into a piece of luck equal to that of stumbling over the rug I never would have found it at all.

I was flashing my light around, about to go back up, when the dim rays picked up a bit of metal and glinted its reflection back at me. I nearly passed it up, thinking it was a bottle cap or the top of a snuff can. But my luck had been so rotten as far as locating anything was concerned that I took a look just to make sure.

It was a half-dollar, partially buried in soft dirt. It was away back, almost against the wall, and under the steps. I picked it up, a nice, shiny, untarnished four-bits. It hadn't lain there long enough to become dulled, I was sure of that. Sure enough to make me flash the light around some more.

I picked them up, one by one. A wallet, well stuffed with money but little else. Just a few cards, a driver's license, the usual stuff. Only these all had one thing in common: they bore the name of Ralph Burnham.

I gathered up the labels I found. A coat label, overcoat label, one from a hat. All initialed. And with the whole thing in my hand I started up the stairs. They were hardly stairs, just notched two-by-four timbers and floor planks across them. There were no risers, just empty space where they would ordinarily be. I reasoned that from the position of the stuff that whoever had thrown it there had simply opened the trapdoor, leaned over, and tossed the stuff through the place where the riser of the step—the top step—would have been.

But I didn't have much time to investigate. Coming up into the bedroom, I almost ran into Saarkinnen. And he was mad.

XV.

I forestalled what I thought he was going to say by thrusting the wallet and labels in to his big hands.

"These don't prove there is a corpse," I said, "but they help."

I went on into the living room and sat down in the easy chair. Mart and Bart had the couch. When Saarkinnen came silently in after me, they moved apart so he could sit between them.

He was as silent as they, gnawing at the stub of a cold cigar and turning the wallet over and over in his hands. The labels he set aside as temporarily unimportant. He gave them to Mart and Bart.

"Where'd you get these?" he asked me.

"Down cellar." I told him how I had discovered the trap door. I didn't add what I was thinking, that Anitra or Burnham and Company would hardly have known about the trap door any more than I. That it must have been someone quite familiar with the place.

"We need these," he said. He wasn't friendly, nor definitely unfriendly, at the moment. The anger I had seen on his face had been shelved for the time being. I saw a chance to keep it away, by getting my licks in first.

"What the devil," I asked, "was the idea of roaring up here with that siren going full blast? I would have had a juicier prize for you if you hadn't scared him away."

"Burnham-Prigwell?" His slow grin mocked me, now that I knew he had known for some time the identity of the Government man.

"No, a gunman," I said to make it sound good and dramatic. "Burnham's chauffeur and probably a pal of the loving Anitra."

He grinned again. "We got that guy whenever we want him. He's staying at the hotel. He and your wife.

Connecting rooms." He looked to see how I was taking that.

It was immaterial to me. I wouldn't have cared had she set up shop and hung a sign out of her window.

"Even so," I said, "with Eve's warning you should have come up quietly."

"What warning? She invited us to a wedding party. We were celebrating."

He pushed himself to his feet suddenly and glared down at me. "And listen, Hallam, it was funny, us kidding you about marrying Eve last night. But we're not so sure we like it now. By God, if you married her to hide behind her skirts I'll break you in two." He demonstrated his capabilities along that line by opening and closing a pair of huge fists under my nose. "And if you are already married to this Anitra—"

I didn't like it. He was too big, too tough, and his authority could throw a lot of weight around.

I said, "She's nothing to me. I never saw her before. Eve knows all about it anyway. I told her."

He took a last savage bite of his cigar and then chucked the stub into the stove. After studying the fire a few seconds he scooped some wood off the floor and put that in the stove.

"You told her," he said. "That means everyone knows about it but me. Why in hell didn't I get my report this morning?"

My grin was a little malicious. "I ran into a guy and he wanted me to come here. By the time I got a chance to call you I was on my way to get married."

He didn't ask me who the guy was, so I deduced Dirkson had contacted him. I said, "Do you want the story of Anitra whatever her name really is?"

"Okay." He turned to the couch and sat staring straight at me. His hands were busy with the wallet, aimlessly turning it back and forth with his fingers.

"You've seen her?" ..

"Yes," he said. "Quite an eyeful."

"She had a marriage certificate," I said. "With my name on it. Dated four years ago, from San Francisco. I don't know how she got it—or anything else about the damned thing. But she has it and she says she's going to exercise her rights as a wife and move in with me—until I give her the clothes."

"Those damned clothes! So?"

"So," I grinned, "that didn't work and she sent her stooge here to bluff them out of me. That flopped. I don't know what they'll do next."

"She really act like your wife?"

"Not at first," I said. "But later she tried to tell me that my two years out of circulation were spent in a bughouse. That I was suffering from partial amnesia and we were really married.

"Then she tried to vamp me." The outmoded word sounded funny to my ears.

"That work?"

He was easier now. The way he said that sounded like his heavy humor. I was opening up to him and he was feeling better toward me.

"No. So—then she pushed me around."

"She's big enough," he admitted. "So?"

"I got mad," I said. "When that happens I forget how scared I am. I hit her and left."

"Yeah," he said. "You owe the hotel for one window. I heard about that." He smiled briefly, then was serious again. "You took a hell of a chance, Hallam. You can get in for bigamy."

"It was Eve's idea," I explained, "to force her hand. If she charges me with bigamy, she'll have to come out in the open and lay everything on the table."

"If that certificate looks good, Hallam, it can lock you up while we're checking."

"I expected that."

His jaw shot forward. "Why'd you marry Eve?"

Tell him half-truths or full truth? I said, "Because I love her."

"You haven't known her very long."

"She hasn't known me very long," I pointed out.

"She fell for a bunch of newspaper articles, not a man," he said stubbornly.

"I'll keep on writing them," I said. "For the *Vinson Record*."

"Letsburg isn't far from here, Hallam. You be good to her or I'll see about it—if you come out of this whole."

Swell, I thought. I marry an orphan who has more pseudo-relatives than an Irish girl has real ones. And all of them just as tough.

"I told you how I feel," I said inadequately.

Saarkinnen rose. "We got work to do before the supper tonight. Bart, you go down cellar and see what you can find. Mart, you come with me. Wait in the hotel for us, Bart."

"You better take it easy, Hallam. Stay out of Bossy's way. She's not happy about all this."

"I thought," I said, "that you came to celebrate."

"This stuff you found makes things look different," he said. "I got to go back to Letsburg." He paused in the doorway. "With these we got something to work on. We've got a body down at the coroner's."

I followed Bart into the cellar. To establish a right to be there, I said, "I'll show you where I found the wallet and stuff."

"Yeah," he said. "Yeah, show me."

I pointed under the stair. "My theory is that the person who threw the stuff into the cellar didn't come downstairs. He just opened the trapdoor, bent over, and tossed it down under the top step."

He looked up at the steps and nodded. "Could be. But I don't reckon many strangers're going to roll rugs up an' find this door by luck. And it seems to me if the body-snatchers had known of it they woulda sneaked the body down here instead of carting it off. This'd be a fine place to hide a body."

I was surprised. Bart seemed to be able to reason. "Where," I asked, "did you find the body?"

"The sheriff found it," Bart said. "In a back yard."

That told me a lot; I said as much.

Bart fixed me with what I took to be a suspicious eye—probably he had learned it by correspondence. "Sure you don't know?"

I assured him not only did I not know but I wasn't sure that there was anything to this body story. And if there was, I said I had no idea how the body had got into a back yard, or anywhere else.

Bart's placid eyes were fixed on my face. "Sarky thought an awful lot of that dog, too. Musta got hold of a dead squirrel. It was poisoned."

I was glad I hadn't bitten. But the rigmarole— Saarkinnen dropping an exit line about a body and leaving Bart to watch my reactions—told me I was still under suspicion. More so than before perhaps, now that I had married Eve.

"You said it was at the coroner's," I reminded him.

"Yep. He's the undertaker too. Sarky's giving the dog a real burial," Bart said. "Besides, he ain't sure it was a dead squirrel that poisoned the dog. It was Morozzi's back yard where he found it." He sucked on his toothpick and watched me without attempt to conceal it. He was looking for reactions, but he was incapable of being subtle about it.

"He thinks the dog was poisoned at Morozzi's?" I asked.

"Well, it seems that way. That was where he caught this Dirkson fellow digging, out at Morozzi's chicken ranch. So Sarky takes a spade and goes out there. Morozzi ain't at home on account of he had to go to Lewiston, Mrs. Morozzi says. So she invites Sarky in as sweet as you please. She's always making eyes at him."

I remembered something. Hadn't Morozzi mentioned that already there was a lot of gossip when he had asked me to forget the affair of the chicken burier?

"Only at Saarkinnen?" I ventured.

Bart grinned knowingly and shook his head. "She likes 'em all," he said. "Morozzi, he's gone a lot. But Sarky don't fall for it. He ain't done more'n smiled enough to get her vote for five years now—since she was big enough to vote. Anyway, she gives him permission to dig around her hen house."

"What did he find?" I asked. I wanted to know. To me, Dirkson was altogether too clever a man. I didn't entirely trust that identification badge of his and I wanted to know if he actually was a Government man. I had an idea it would prove something if Saarkinnen had struck pay dirt with his shovel.

"Well, he didn't dig," Bart said. "He found his dog instead. He was cut up about it and he raised hell with Mrs. Morozzi. But she said, no, there wasn't anything she knew about it."

I thought that over. I wasn't very well acquainted in these parts, but it seemed to me that if something was buried at the Morozzi place, something that Dirkson was interested in, Mr. or Mrs. Morozzi would have to be aware of it and connected in some way. He was a salesman and gone a lot of the time. That made it logical, to me, that she might know something. A woman who ran a chicken farm wouldn't have much time to spend away from home. And if she was home a lot she would know what was going on at her own place.

My deductions worked out to what I thought was a clever idea. And the sooner I acted on it the better, I felt. I got up and took a towel. "Mind waiting while I take a bath?"

"Go to it. Man ought to wash on his wedding night, seems to me."

I departed with my towel, leaving Bart's gem of philosophy hanging in the air.

XVI.

In the hotel, I came to an open door. There was a nice, modern bath inside. The door next to it was closed but I could hear someone moving about. I took a chance. "Eve?"

There were footsteps, quick ones. Eve opened the door. I was glad it wasn't Adam's room or Bossy would probably have broken my neck for trying to see my wife without permission. That was the way I felt about Bossy. She seemed as fiercely protective of Eve as a she-wolf of her pups. And a lot more dangerous. There was so much of Bossy.

"Darling," Eve said in a relieved voice. "I've been wondering about—was she in your house?"

"No," I said. "It was that blond chauffeur boy. He wanted the clothes too. Only he had a gun instead of papers."

"I saw Sarky go in," she said, "so I stayed here."

She stepped aside and I went into her room. It was a nice room, but rather plain. There were the usual frilly feminine things about and on the walls a pair of tasteful prints. One whole wall was taken up with a well filled bookcase. I liked that about her. The bedspread was wrinkled as if she had been lying down. I sat on the edge of the bed, since I didn't suppose another wrinkle would matter now. She sat beside me.

"Tell me," she commanded.

She smoked a cigarette while I told her everything that had occurred, including my idea. She nodded occasionally and looked completely nonplussed when I mentioned that the identification papers we supposed had come from the corpse were in the name of Burnham.

"But he's the one who signed my check," she said.

"I think," I told her, "we might have a fount of

information. Mrs. Morozzi seems to be slightly on the nymphomaniac side. If you'll trust me, darling, I'll go see what I can find out."

"Alone?" She shook her head.

"Alone," I said. "Only I want you along. I mean I want you to snoop around that chicken house where Dirkson was caught while I interview Mrs. Morozzi."

"If you need help, yell," she answered. She crushed her cigarette in an ashtray and looked at me. "She's quite attractive, Tom."

I murmured the necessary assurances and kissed her. She seemed satisfied, so we got up and she went after a coat. "How do we get out of here?" I asked. "Bart is in back and I don't want this to be common knowledge just yet."

"Wait here," she said. "I'll get the Moon and bring it around front. I'll keep it throttled down, but you'll be able to hear it. When you do, dash out through the lobby. Come here and I'll show you the door." She took me into the hallway and pointed to a door at its extreme end. "That way," she said. "Then run out and climb in."

I agreed, kissed her again, and settled down to wait. Inside of five minutes I heard the Moon's deep voice stuttering out front. I went into the hall, out the end door, and quickly across the chilly, dim lobby to the street.

It was nearing dark when I clambered into the car beside Eve. She turned the headlights on only after we had left the edge of town. The roads were slippery but she drove as fast as if they had been dry and clean of snow. We didn't go quite into Letsburg but swung onto a back road about a mile from town. It arced us around so that we came to Morozzi's without having gone near the town itself. The place consisted of a little white bungalow covered with brown stems of vines across the front porch. There seemed to be about two acres, most of which was covered with chicken houses. A good distance away Eve throttled the car to a murmur and then pulled into a clump of timber and cut the motor.

"We'll go on foot," she said. "And do be careful, Tom. She isn't safe."

I grinned at that, kissed her with sufficient violence to dispel any doubts she might have, and took off down the road. There was a light in the front room when I reached the little porch, so I walked up quietly and peered under the half-drawn shade.

Mrs. Morozzi was alone. She was sitting in a deep chair near an oil heater. I could see her fingers moving as if she were sewing. Otherwise all I could notice was a mass of very dark hair and one slippered foot.

I knocked on the door. I heard her stir and a moment later she opened the door. She looked out at me while I blinked to get my eyes accustomed to the light.

"Yes?" Her voice was warm but without the suggestive huskiness of Anitra's. When my eyes had adjusted themselves to the light I could see that she was indeed fairly nice-looking. But no knockout. Her face was round and pouty, with prominent moist lips. Her eyes were big and dark under a mass of black hair. She wore a clean housedress and it was tight enough to reveal a nice figure if you like them chunky.

"I'm from the newspaper," I said. I produced one of my old press cards. I had carried a number of them, all fakes but the one from the *Mail,* and supposedly made out by everything from the *New York Times* to the *Tokyo Advertiser.* They were decorated with an equally large assortment of names. I had held onto them as a matter of sentiment and for something to reminisce over, but until now I had given no thought to using them. The one I handed her was made out to John Boettiger from the *Seattle P. I.*

She looked at it and handed it back to me. Evidently she didn't read beyond the Letsburg and Vinson papers because she entertained no suspicion that it was a gag. She simply said, "What do you want?"

"An interview," I said. "And later, pictures, Mrs. Morozzi. I'm travelling to get the average American's view on things. I understand there has been trouble here—or so your sheriff tells me. I thought your point of view would be interesting."

I smiled, a little knowingly I hoped. "Besides, anything offered by a pretty woman is eaten up by the readers."

She smiled back and asked me in. It was as simple as that. I took the davenport. It was a so-called modernistic piece. The whole room was done that way, the style of a few years back. It seemed out of place in these semi-wilds, but you could see she liked it.

She sat down near me and waited. Her eyes were fixed expectantly on my face. The way she had curled herself on the couch exposed a little of her skin above the rolled top of her stocking and below the edge of her skirt. Every now and then she would touch the tip of her tongue to her already moist lips. The more I talked the sultrier she looked. I began to believe that the mere sight of masculinity was an aphrodisiac to her.

I gave her a line about the man her husband had had arrested and then I asked what she knew about it. I even went so far as to take a notebook from my pocket and get ready to take notes.

"Nothing," she said to me. "I was getting dinner. My husband said he heard something outside. He went to the back porch and listened. The chickens were squawking and he heard them. He took his flashlight and went outside."

"He wasn't afraid?"

"No."

"Would you have been?"

She smiled at me—not in answer to my question. "I like the dark," she said.

I scribbled furiously. "Then he found this man. Did he have a gun?"

"My husband didn't talk to him," she said. "He ran back and called the sheriff. He didn't even use his flashlight. He could see that there was a man there and he was digging in the chicken house."

"The chicken house? You have only one?" I looked surprised. "I understood you were a well known chicken rancher, Mrs. Morozzi."

The way she looked made me realize all I had to do was reach out a hand and touch her and Mr. Morozzi would once more be a cuckold.

"There are twelve houses," she said. "Besides the broiler pens. This was in the first house. It's just a little ways back of the porch."

I nodded and scribbled again. "And when the sheriff came, the man was still there."

"The sheriff's office isn't a mile from here," she said.

"Did the man fight?"

"No, he went with them quietly."

"Did you see him?"

"No," she said.

"You were afraid?"

"I am never afraid," she said. Her eyes weren't on her subject, but fixed on me. The answers seemed more or less automatic—something to fill in until this tiresome part of my visit should be concluded.

I asked a few more questions, pointless, and received the same type of answer. By this time I thought Eve had had enough time to do what scouting she needed to and I got up.

"Thank you," I said. "I'll want to have some pictures taken later—if you don't mind." She got up with me and was just a little in the lead when we reached the door. "Pictures of you in your house and maybe out with the chickens."

"You'll come—alone?" She was very close, between me and the door. I seemed to be a prize she didn't want to lose, nor to defer until later. She touched me with her body and put her hands out. Nothing subtle about Mrs. Morozzi.

"Sure," I agreed. I reached for the door. "With my camera."

Her hands went up and got me by the back of the neck. She started hauling to pull me to her level. There is nothing more ridiculous than a man resisting a kiss. Yet I didn't feel much like setting off Morozzi dynamite by kissing her and then trying to retire. And I couldn't stand forever with my back stiff.

"Do you know a blond man who drives a big Cadillac?" I asked. It was the first question I could think of that might jar her. I mentioned the chauffeur rather than Anitra or Fatso Burnham because I could see him using this woman simply by smiling promises at her.

It jarred her, all right. She backed off and stared at me, her nostrils flaring. "Who are you?"

"You saw my card," I said. I had my hand on the door, had it open, and backed outside. She did the damnedest thing then. She started screaming. I could hear her screams until I was nearly to the Moon. And how fast I got there! I ran as rapidly as the snowy landscape and my lungs would let me.

Eve had the motor started when I reached the car. I stumbled onto the seat and panted. She picked up speed and we headed back for Vinson.

"Did you have to fight her off?" she chuckled.

"Hear the screams?"

"Faintly," she said. "I thought they were yours at first."

I told her the whole thing. "I hope I gave you enough time," I ended.

"You did," she said. "For a preliminary survey, anyway. It's odd, isn't it, that she would get so upset when you mentioned the chauffeur?"

"It proves she knows something," I said. "What did you find?"

"Loose dirt," Eve said. "There were a few chickens that hadn't gone to roost when I first got there. I watched them and they were all scratching in the same spot. The ground is frozen pretty well and when they find soft dirt they go for it.

"I let them get to roost and then went in quietly. I had better luck than the man Sarky caught. They didn't squawk."

"Did you dig?"

"Look." She showed me her hands; they were dirty. "I couldn't find a shovel. But I scraped at the dirt with my hands. And it's loose and freshly turned, too. Not frozen even as it would be from last night's snap. A space about six by three."

"Sounds like a hole was dug for a coffin."

"Yes," she agreed, "or for our corpse without benefit of coffin, maybe."

XVII.

The party was like all other Vinson social life, held in the kitchen. We clustered around the big table in much the same order as on the previous night. Eve looked quite lovely in a soft green dress of some smooth, light material. It clung to her in those places she had for dresses to cling, and it set off the beauty of her eyes and hair and that entrancing slice of red mouth.

There was something else about her that it took me a few moments to realize. She had done her hair differently. Instead of the bun at the nape of her neck, she had left it loose so that it flowed around her shoulders. It gave her a much softer, more fragile, childish look.

She wasn't one of these girls who push a man away because she's afraid he will ruin her make-up. When I came through the door she was there to meet me, and no lipstick would have been proof against such an onslaught.

Everyone laughed while I squirmed as she wiped the traces of the kiss off my mouth, and if any tension had been forming the laughter shut the door on it.

In Vinson the social custom seemed to decree eating first and talking afterward. When we were all seated and before anyone had time to think up the customary wedding jokes, Bossy had the table loaded and the eating got under way.

The food was good, plentiful, and thirst-provoking. To take care of the thirst, Bossy broke out a case of steinies and we had beer.

After most of the food was gone, she brought in small wine glasses, followed by a bottle of port.

"There's an old German saying," Bossy said, "anyway

I heard it from the German, maybe it's Scandinavian—
'Beer after wine makes man a swine, but wine after beer
and all is good cheer!' So don't refuse this."

Quite evidently a special treat and Bossy intended to
see that everyone did appreciate it. Adam certainly did.
The old boy had gorged on food and gurgled beer as
though he had never seen either before. And the way his
eyes lighted and a look of happiness appeared on that
ghoul-like countenance was an incongruous sight. It
made me think that this wine was a really rare event in
his life. Saarkinnen offered him a cigar and the old man
stretched his hand longingly toward it, all the while
looking at Bossy's face set like a steel trap.

"Now," Saarkinnen said comfortably, "Eve doesn't get
married every day, Bossy. One won't hurt."

"One, then," she said grudgingly. "But no more."

Adam literally snatched the cigar from Saarkinnen's
hand before Bossy could change her mind. When he saw
she was doing other things, he sighed relievedly, and put
it in his mouth. Then he took it out and gently licked—
actually licked it—here and there. He savored it that way
half the evening, licking and smelling and biting it ever
so gently before he ever touched a match to it.

Eve told me, "Adam loves cigars and he smoked them
all the time until Bossy and the local doctor, who's
doctoring in the cavalry now, decided they were bad for
the old man's health. I don't think they would hurt him."

For the second time I was reminded of Adam's longing
for the forbidden fruit, and I tucked the knowledge away
for future use.

With the wine the party loosened a little and talking
began. Eve, snuggled close to me, made it bearable. The
conversation was mostly of neighbors and the local trifles
about which I knew nothing and cared less.

It was a good three hours after we had come in when
we heard the sound of the car in the alley back of the
carriage shed. I should say cars, for first we heard the
tinny sound of an old, small motor, then drowning it out

the throaty roar of a big car.

Eve's unbelievably quick ears caught the sounds, I believe, before anyone else's. I felt her stiffen beside me, and then she tried to relax without much success.

"The Cad?" I asked in a low voice.

She nodded. "I'm sure of it."

"What about the other one?"

She shook her head after the manner of a shrug. I said, "Bart's Model T?" And she didn't have to say anything for me to know I was right.

I looked at Saarkinnen, who was holding forth to Bossy and Adam about some obscene and evidently useless local cow.

He was talking to them, but he had his eye on us and his attitude suggested he was listening outside.

I remembered earlier in the evening and wondered if Saarkinnen had had something to do with whatever was coming. I felt sure that something was, otherwise everyone would have been up at the sound of strange motors in the backyard.

But no one outside of Eve gave any sign of having heard. Not even Bart, who certainly should have recognized the sound of his own car.

I didn't have long to wait. Eve was trying to look unconcerned and doing a poor job of it when the sound of quick footsteps on the porch steps stiffened her as taut as a piano wire.

Bossy looked up and made a move to get up. But the footsteps gave her no chance. Almost before I could swivel in my chair and face the back door, it opened.

Anitra walked in, all smiles and very beautiful. She was dressed completely out of tune with her locale, but it wasn't anything that would rub too much the wrong way.

She wore a rich, black fur coat, open to show that black and white slack suit that helped out on every curve. There was a black and white scarf over her blonde hair, peasant style. She had on a little too much make-up but in that light she could stand it.

"There you are!" she said brightly. Her lips were smiling and her throaty voice had all the stops out. "I didn't see any light in our little house so I came over here. Introduce me, Tom."

She came over and touched my arm with gloved fingers. I recalled something about her and grinned. Her face changed ever so slightly, so I knew she didn't like the grin. I was pretty sure this was Saarkinnen's doing and that everyone but me had been tipped off to what was coming. Eve's tenseness explained that. She couldn't have been so perturbed unless she had known about it.

And from the way Anitra was acting I suspected she did not know what had happened to me that day.

I grinned at her. Turning to the others, I introduced them one by one, omitting Eve. Then I said, "This is Miss Anitra—" and let it hang. "She's staying at the hotel in Letsburg."

Anitra's face was angry; she was looking not at me but at Saarkinnen, and the look seemed to say, "Why didn't you warn me?"

I was enjoying myself, and in the close stillness that followed I threw my last coal on the fire.

"Oh, darling, this is Anitra." I nodded toward Eve. "My wife. You came just in time to help us celebrate. This is our wedding party."

Anitra smiled the sweet cat smile of a woman ready to use an axe on someone. I had to hand it to her, she was an actress.

"Tom! Married?"

"Today," I said. My grin dared her to do anything.

That is where I should have known better. A woman who will pull such a colossal bluff on an absolute stranger in the first place isn't going to stop all at once.

"My dear," she said pityingly to Eve, "this is a shame. Poor Tom, you know, has these spells. I've had trouble before. But never like this—never this serious. Why, Mr. Burnham was kind enough to lend me his car and his chauffeur tonight to move my things to Tom's. You see,

I'm his wife."

I heard Saarkinnen suck in his breath and Eve give a little gasp and tighten her fingers on my arm.

I was in it now for sure. But no worse than I should have expected. Somehow when Eve had explained the plan that morning I hadn't really believed Anitra would back her bluff.

She was, and with a vengeance.

I said angrily, "Well, tell your brother or lover or whoever that blond bum is to take your stuff out of my place. You're no more my wife than Bossy is."

"Tom, dear . . ." Her voice oozed worry and contrition. "I know it must be embarrassing, but when this spell is over you'll thank me—when you're in your right mind again."

I took a deep breath and hung onto Eve to keep from heaving a chair at the bitch.

"Saarkinnen," I said, "that fancy lingerie we found in my place belonged to this woman."

She interrupted. "Of course, when I finally found you, Tom, I put my things in. Where did you put them?"

"You know damned well," I said, "I didn't put them. Your things! You couldn't have worn that much underwear if you were in the business of selling it." I didn't say what "it" was. "And a hell of a fuss you've made over the clothes if they were just yours for wearing. Threatening me and then sending your 'brother' over with a gun after them."

"What's that, Hallam?" Saarkinnen asked me.

"A gun," I said. "That fancy pants who drives the big Cadillac came over with a gun to scare those clothes out of me. Your siren chased him away."

"Oh, yes, you told me." And he sat down, seemingly uninterested.

That stumped me. Here I had proved, I thought, that this woman was some sort of crook, and not even the sheriff had anything to say.

I looked at Anitra then. It was her turn to grin now,

but she wasn't taking advantage of her opportunity. Instead, she was looking at the sheriff.

"You'll have to arrest Tom," she said. Her voice had that lugubrious hypocrisy that suggested this was a painful duty but it must be done. For my own good, of course. It was all there. She went on and added a little more drama to her tone. "I've protected him all that I can. This is just too much."

"On a bigamy charge?" Saarkinnen asked her. He looked bland and unimpressed by the dramatics. Beside me I could feel Eve trembling and stiffening as the situation worked on her nerves.

"Yes," Anitra said. She smiled a wan smile. "There's nothing I can do now, is there?"

Eve started to rise, and Anitra turned just a little and looked at her. The smile changed almost imperceptibly. But enough to send Eve sinking back into her chair. She had her teeth clenched hard and her hands doubled up into little fists. I expected some sort of an explosion any moment.

It came, from Bossy. She rose as rapidly as her tremendous bulk would let her and strode to Anitra. She put one hand on Anitra's arm. Her face was a design of fury in fat. I couldn't see her eyes but I could imagine them.

"You lie," she said. Her voice was high and harsh. "Get out! Get away—stay away." She dropped her hands. Anitra rubbed her arm and looked at Saarkinnen. He was making patterns on the table top with his fingertips. Bossy moved a fraction of an inch—forward. Anitra took one look and fled. The screen door banged loudly behind her.

I started after her, but Bossy blocked me.

"Let her go," Saarkinnen said. "All she needs is enough rope."

"But she and that chauffeur will go through my house," I said weakly.

"So? Anything to take but beer?"

"No," I admitted. I remembered Bossy's defense of me. Rather belatedly I said, "Thanks. I appreciate it."

She looked at me and there was no softness in her. "It was for Eve," she said bluntly, and returned to her chair.

"Besides," Saarkinnen said, referring to Anitra, "another car drove up. Maybe he'll take care of things."

I wasn't so sure of that, but I didn't argue with the sheriff. Suddenly I was filled with uneasiness. I had to get Eve alone. There were things I had to find out and things I had to do. I was buzzing with ideas, none of them bridegroomish. But they would have to look that way to pry us from the now silent group.

So I said as coyly as I could stomach, "Shall I carry you over the threshold, darling?"

Eve squeezed my hand. "I believe in you, Tom," she whispered. Aloud she said, "I've been hoping you would."

When we walked out, the snow had stopped and the moon was shining. It was cold and beautiful. I hoped Dirkson or Saarkinnen or fear had chased Anitra and her pal away.

"I didn't hear the cars drive away," Eve said thoughtfully.

"Not even Saarkinnen's," I added.

XVIII.

We ran across a snow-covered, moonlit world toward the dark spot that was the cabin. I could see no cars as I peered past the carriage shed, and that reassured me a little. Perhaps we just hadn't heard them move away.

"Even if they are still around," Eve's voice said, "as long as they aren't in the house we won't let them disturb us, will we?" Her voice sounded wistful.

We had reached the porch and stopped a little for breath. I grinned down at her. "A hell of a way to spend a wedding night—with one ear cocked for unwanted visitors."

"All visitors are unwanted on a wedding night," Eve smiled.

We went up the steps. I held out my arm and stopped her. "Just a second," I said. And with a show of bravery I definitely did not feel, I opened the door and stumbled into the dark front room. I didn't waste any time trying to see in that darkness. I made violent grabs in the air until my fingers closed over the drop-cord of the light. One hard yank and the darkness was gone, leaving me blinded and blinking. That went away after a moment and I saw that so far we were alone.

The bedroom was untenanted also. I had a minute of regret that I had not left it in better condition. Maybe Eve wouldn't mind too much.

She was shivering on the porch when I returned. "All clear," I announced, and then, though I scarcely felt up to it, I picked her up and staggered across the threshold in the prescribed manner.

Eve was not a particularly small girl, and I was much too light and reedy for much of such chivalry. But I did manage to make the couch before she started slipping.

Then I let her go all at once. She gasped as I dumped her unceremoniously on the cushions.

"Rat," she said. She reached up, pulled me down beside her, and kissed me with such thoroughness that I nearly forgot there were important things scheduled for this night.

On the excuse of shutting the doors and building the fire, I got up. Eve watched me idly for a moment, then rose too. The little overnight bag she had clung to all during her ride in my arms and subsequent fall, she laid on the couch and opened.

It was my turn to watch her. It was probably the most peculiar luggage ever carried by a new bride. First she brought out a wooly green bathrobe and slippers to match it. These she laid to one side. They were followed by a fifth of whiskey which she solemnly placed on the drainboard.

She bent again to dip into the bag. "Tom, will you fix us a drink?"

I made two whiskeys, thinned with icy tap water, and when I brought them to the couch she had the bag shut and set on the floor. In her hand she held a faintly familiar white envelope.

"This is what you wanted to see, wasn't it, Tom? My legacy?"

I sat on the couch, set the glasses down, and began fumbling for my pipe. "Yes," I said. It was hard to know how to begin. This was what I wanted but I hadn't realized I was so transparent.

Eve handed me the envelope. I gave her a whiskey. She raised the glass. "To an understanding, Tom. Because without it we can't have a happy marriage."

I got my glass and drank with her. She said, "Let me get warm with this drink and I won't be so tongue-tied. I have a sort of confession to make." She nodded at the envelope. "Go ahead."

I passed her the cigarettes, lit my pipe, and then opened the envelope.

There was the two-thousand dollar check made out to Eve Vinson and signed by Ralph Burnham. Setting it aside, I looked at the sheaf of papers. Then I looked at Eve. She wore a small, tilted smile but her eyes were worried.

"What the hell?" I handed the papers to her. They were no good to me; all of them were blank. "That photo of Prigwell is missing," I said.

"There isn't any photo. I'll explain it all later, Tom. I just wanted you to see what was in the envelope. There was one more thing, but I've been carrying that with me."

She dug into the front of her dress and came up with a sheet of paper folded into a small pad. I opened it and smoothed out the creases.

It was quite a shock. The print was in ink, plain block letters, undistinguished by any particular marks. It read, "Watch this guy Hallam. He's a snoop." That was all; no signature, nothing more. I handed it back to her.

"Yes, keep it safe, sweet," I said. "We wouldn't want everyone to know how dangerous I am."

Her face was so full of hurt that I was ashamed of my sarcasm. She said, "I suppose I'm going at this backward. But I haven't the courage yet to tell you things." She took a good pull at her drink, another, and the glass was empty.

"More?"

She nodded and I refilled her glass. She didn't seem to need much of this. She took two swallows, set the glass down, and lit a second cigarette from the first one.

"Tom, I don't know what you'll think after I tell you this. That's why I'm telling you now—before anything—so if you want to, you can get an annulment by claiming there has been no consummation of the marriage."

"Whoa," I said. "Let me judge that, will you? After all, I'm no baby. I knew something was wrong when I married you." I was glad now of Anitra's visit, if it had shocked Eve into telling me what I would have had to ask."

Her smile was pallid. "It's just this, Tom. When I wrote and asked you to come here and work on the paper I had no ulterior motives. I had really fallen in love with your work and I did want to see what you were like. And I had an idea that two years in a sanitarium had financially embarrassed you, so it was half charity, half business.

"But after I became involved and I knew you were coming, I got selfish. Instead of writing and telling you to stay away, I figured out a way of using you and possibly saving myself."

Her eyes were bleak as she faced me. "As a husband you wouldn't have to tesitfy against your wife."

"Is that why you married me?"

"That was my original intention," she admitted. "But I married you because I thought—and think—I'm in love with you. I don't expect you to believe me."

"What did you do?" I asked. "You sound like a combination murderess, arsonist, and rapist. You didn't do Prigwell in, did you?"

"No. I haven't killed anyone. And not Prigwell especially. There is no real person by that name. No one I ever heard of!"

That was almost too much to take. To date, Dirkson had used the name and a small corpse seemed to have claimed it. I had heard both Eve and Burnham's chauffeur use it. And now she was telling me the name was fiction.

She was talking again. "It's a name that was made up. It caused quite a stir in Seattle when I was in college, and I had hoped it had reached this far east and stuck in Sarky's mind—but maybe I'd better start at the beginning."

She took a sip of the whiskey; I made myself another. I had a feeling that I was going to need it.

"It started very innocently when I was a sophomore in college," Eve went on. "I was at the adolescent age when the burning problems of the world first hit me. All of the things men devote their lives to fighting: race prejudice, poverty, bad working conditions, too much wealth in the hands of too few—they struck me all at once and made a violent impression on my unformed and distinctly rustic mind."

She smiled, a little bitterly. "I went overboard for a while. I joined the various liberal campus movements, wrote wild editorials that the student paper of course wouldn't publish, and even made a few soap-box speeches on May Day. You know how it goes.

"It wore off, as such things do. That is, the volcano and lack of restraint wore off. By the next year I had begun to realize that fervent speeches can't remake a world.

"But I was still immersed in the desire to do something, and I had attracted the attention of a few extremists. We formed a society. Very small, select, and secret. I was to do most of the writing; we were to print a small newspaper. The thing was in reality a scandal sheet, a blackmail scheme, if you will. I see that now. But at that time it was to me a tool with which to build a finer society.

"We were, as the leader said, to learn how to equalize humanity by practicing first on the wealthier, more snobbish students in school, and later branch out to the more reactionary townspeople and the most vicious of factory owners.

"And that is what I believed." She stopped and gulped nervously at the whiskey. "I was a fairly simple-minded country child, I guess. I wrote those nasty little articles on certain students, letting the others do the research. Little gibes, hints about their morals, nasty cracks, threats, all the muck that could be raked up.

"And I thought I was doing a fine job. I was smug and smart! Then we branched out into little threatening letters to people of the city. Few and cautious, but they were potential dynamite.

"It was only after we publicly exploded that I found

out what was going on under my nose. I was being used as the fall guy. I was doing the writing, and the others of the little group were using the stuff I wrote—actually blackmailing with it. And the whole thing was organized by an outsider, someone I never knew or saw, but who with the others of this group had a clever racket and were quite well protected."

"Good Lord," I said, "that's as old as the hills—and as rotten. I uncovered a few little messes of that type myself when I was working. But no one was such a dupe as you!"

"Dope, you mean," she said without smiling. "I was pretty stupid. And how I kept from being caught I'll never know. There was a big flurry by the police, a mild sort of an investigation that made smoke and noise only, and when no one else came forward—those who had been blackmailed, I mean— it died out.

"I tried to quit, but the others refused to let me by threatening to expose me. They also reminded me that we had pledged to stick together. Which was all hokum but quite effective at the time.

"However, before we could do too much damage, they left school—because their boss decided that the racket was no longer profitable—and disappeared. That left me free, of course."

"Then you're still liable for blackmail charges?" I asked.

She nodded glumly. "Worse. They managed to retrieve some of the stuff I wrote and can hold it over me. And do."

"Anitra and the chauffeur," I said. "My God, Eve!"

"Yes," she said. "Anitra, whose name is Irma Mullen, really; his is Raymond Parkman. They were the others I spoke of."

"And Burnham is the mysterious organizer?"

"I don't know. I never knew who he was. We always referred to him as Joseph Prigwell, and that's the way all the letters were signed. I really never heard of a Burnham."

I finished my second whiskey.

"So," I said, sounding like Saarkinnen even to myself, "when they decided to use Vinson as a headquarters for smuggling, they contacted you?"

She nodded miserably. "I had almost forgotten about the whole thing—years can cover a lot of things."

"But that check for two thousand. Eve—you haven't been in with them actually?"

"That," she said, "is rent, I suppose. Rent for my properties. They'll use the empty brick buildings as storehouses. But I'm not that stupid. I won't cash the check."

I saw that. If she did, she was involved simply by the action. As it was, she might be able to keep fairly clear if they should be caught.

I thought of Dirkson and I felt sick. I looked at Eve and she looked better than ever to me. Her misery reached out and took hold of me. I still didn't know just how I was to have been used as a sucker, but I was damned if I believed it any idea of hers.

And I knew I was in love at the same instant that I knew that Eve was in more danger, far more, of the law than I.

XIX.

"So you see," Eve continued, "I'm in a nasty position. That check was a trap, and the blank paper a warning, not the first I've received. But it was the first time that Raymond visited me personally."

"You did a lovely bit of acting," I said. "I sensed that something was wrong but I had no idea you knew him." There were a lot of things I had to find out, and if this mood of hers lasted I might get the answer.

"Why did you identify the man as Joseph Prigwell?"

"Because," she said promptly, "I was trying, without daring to expose them or myself, to recall to you and Sarky those letters. I thought it might give you a clue. If either of you had remembered the Prigwell case it would have set the thing in motion."

"You were taking a chance on being discovered," I pointed out.

"Some, but I thought it was a chance worth taking—either that or spending the rest of my life knowing Vinson was a smugglers' hideout, worrying about discovery by the Federal men."

She looked completely and utterly miserable, but I forced myself not to think of that; there were still things I felt I could—and needed—to find out.

"Why did Anitra pretend to be my wife?"

"I honestly don't know," Eve said, and I could see it was the truth.

"But how did they ever find out I was coming to Vinson?"

"Through me," Eve said. "Not directly, but through me just the same. They got into the newspaper office at night and broke into my correspondence file. They read my letters to you and you to me, accepting the job and everything. I suppose they concocted a scheme to use you. They're so good at that."

I shook my head. "I can see some of it now—there were evidently four of them. Anitra or Irma, Raymond what's-his-name—"

"Parkman."

"Yes, Parkman. And the man you called Prigwell and our fat, sleepy friend, Burnham. He may be this leader if he's the one who signs the checks. It seems to me Sarky could do a little investigating of him.

"But all of it," I went on, "doesn't give them a motive for murdering one of their number."

"No," Eve said in an odd voice, "it doesn't. It gives *me* a motive."

"But not unless you were a fool or panicky," I pointed out.

"I've been both in my life."

"Recently?"

"Fool enough to—" She flushed and looked defiantly at me. "Fool enough to fall for you, Tom."

"We're both fools then. It's a reciprocal proposition."

"You should hate me." She wasn't being dramatic, either.

"Or you me. How do you know I didn't marry you to hide from Anitra's trap?"

"Did you?" Her smile was closer to normal than it had been in some time.

"No, but Saarkinnen seemed to have that idea."

"Sarky's a very protective sort, Tom. He's known me since I was a baby—before that, if it's possible to be acquainted with a coming event."

"He seems like a decent enough person," I admitted. "Couldn't you tell him this, get his help?"

She shook her head very seriously. "No, I couldn't. Sarky just isn't the kind of person you can tell. I don't mean he would have me prosecuted. He wouldn't. That's just the trouble. He'd pretend on the surface that everything was the same between us, that I'd had a rotten deal and all that. But inside, Sarky would feel differently toward me, and be eating away at himself because by not turning me in he would he compromising himself.

"Do I make it clear? I feel awfully muddled."

"Clear enough. Sarky's an idealist, then, in his way."

"Completely, violently honest," she said.

"Am I the only person, then, you've told this to, Eve?"

"Bossy. She's been my confidant since I could talk. Bossy would die before she'd say anything at all to anyone."

I remembered Bossy's fierceness and laughed, a bit shakily. "She'll protect you, don't worry about that."

We lapsed into silence, Eve nursing her glass between the palms of her hands. I was trying to piece things together, to get a few questions answered for my own satisfaction. Trying, too, to keep away from an idea, a suspicion, really, that kept cropping up in my mind.

This, I thought inanely, was one hell of a way to spend a wedding night. Sitting on a couch and lost in reverie. Frightened, both of us.

I was genuinely concerned for Eve. Because I could see that no matter how things went she could become embroiled. If the body were never found, Dirkson's investigation could still unearth all this past nastiness, and if it were found and the murder solved, the same thing could happen.

But I had an idea, stemming from other ideas, that we would be better off if it weren't found.

It was a big risk, and akin to sitting on dynamite, to be quiet and passive and wonder if and when the police would stumble on that body. And sooner or later they would start to hunt for it. Dirkson evidently had seen it. And if he didn't do the finding, he might activate Saarkmnen sufficiently so he would.

That brought me up hard. I knew the answer, yet I hated to put it into so many words in my own mind. I did finally, and admitted that the safest bet was for me to

locate that corpse and hide it so no one would ever find it.
The whole idea made me a little sick at my stomach.

It had it in mind to explain this to Eve, to break
through the melancholy that seemed to have formed a
hard shell around her. If she reacted somewhat as I did to
things, then action such as hunting the body would entail
would relieve her to an extent.

She evidently caught me looking at her. She glanced
up sharply.

"I've been wondering, Tom—the whiskey's gone to my
head and I'm all muddled—but what about those cars?"

I had forgotten I "No one's come," I said. "Yet I'm sure
they didn't drive away—maybe I'd better look around a
bit." It was sheer bravado, the desire of the male to show
his prowess before the female. The thought of actually
going outside in the darkness was enough to throw me
into a funk. Especially now, when I knew these were no
escaped lunatics we were dealing with but that peculiar
and desperate class of people who are intelligent but still
beyond the law.

"I'm going with you," Eve said. And before I could
make the usual protests to cover my relief at having
company, she added: "I need the air, and besides I don't
want to stay in here alone."

"I feel foolish," I said, "but I wish I had a gun." I did
have my flashlight and I was stuffing it in my overcoat
pocket as we moved toward the door.

Eve smiled wisely and tucked her hand into mine.
"Darling, I do believe you're twice as scared as I am."

"I know damned well I am," I assured her. "But I don't
know what at."

"That's why you're scared," she said philosophically. A
hell of a time to be philosophical!

It was cold outside, cold and clear and very still. The
moon through the stark branches of the leafless fruit
trees made black finger like patterns on the heaped snow.
The evergreen shadows were less delicate, more inclined
to mass, and because of the hugeness of them I decided

they would make fine hiding places.

Eve took deep breaths. "The air is good; I was getting tight in there. Not happy tight, but moodily, feeling sorry for myself and vaguely angry with the world. Now I'm ever so much better."

While she prattled on we went down the steps to the walk and cut across toward the carriage shed. The snow was well frozen and our feet made squeaking sounds on it as we walked.

I didn't know what to expect and as we neared the alley and the huge black shadow made by the shed I was ready to find anything.

There was nothing.

A surprise, even a pleasant one, can be an awful let-down when it first hits you. I gaped up and down the alley. There were tire tracks easily visible, but no signs of the cars that had made them.

Eve gave a hysterical little giggle. "Now what?"

"I know damned well," I said, "that we didn't just miss hearing those cars drive off. They're gone—but, damn it—" I stopped. It was hopeless; it didn't make sense. If my stubborn conviction was right and we hadn't simply overlooked their going, it was impossible.

"They went some place," Eve said.

I went into the alley and flashed my light on the tracks. There were other tracks as well, imprinted over the car tracks. In that light they were faint but definite.

"Someone," I said, calling Eve over, "has been doing a lot of stomping around here or—"

She looked closely, got down on one knee and looked again. Then, standing, she nodded solemnly to me. "Or," she said, "the car was pushed away from here." Her voice was very low, as if there might be someone hiding in the forest that stretched so close to us.

Now why in hell would anyone do that?

"From the looks of those tire marks," I said, "it was the Cad. How about Bart's T?"

"Bart's T?"

I had forgotten she was not supposed to know about Dirkson. The news wouldn't make her feel any better, but it certainly wouldn't be fair not to tell her that there was a Government man investigating the smugglers. Besides, it was too hard on me to remember that I was supposed to keep my mouth shut.

So I told her.

"That was Bart's T we saw today, then," she said, "when we were getting ready to drive my car away."

"It was," I said. "Dirkson was peering around inside my place to see what he could find."

Eve shivered. "I'm cold. Let's start moving."

We hunted around for the tracks of the model T, but we couldn't find them anywhere. That was putting it on a little too thick! I said, "Let's follow the tracks of the Cad. If we don't find something soon I'm going inside and drink myself into a stupor."

"Not a full stupor, I hope," Eve said caressingly. She squeezed my arm.

I returned the squeeze absently. My mind was far from the gallantries expected of a groom. I was hunting for something. Yet I had no real idea what it was nor what reason I had for looking.

But that didn't stop me from a frantic feeling of intensity. Sucking too much cold air into my lungs, I bent as low as I could, and with the flashlight on the car tracks I started tracing those broad, footprint-smeared tire marks.

I didn't trace far. I had the feeling that I wasn't going in a straight line, and when I stopped and looked up I found my nose inches from the carriage shed. I was about at the middle. There were four stalls. I had the far end, Eve the one nearest to the hotel driveway. This stall would be next to mine.

Eve was laughing. She put her hand over her mouth to stifle the sounds, but they burst around and through her fingers.

"Oh, Tom, you looked so funny! So God-awful funny.

And you nearly ran your mick face square into the door!"

It was hardly funny to me; I was too excited.

I said impatiently, "Do you keep this locked?"

She came up to me then, her laughter subsiding to a last choking gurgle.

"That isn't our padlock. The one next to my stall has a lock on it, but it's broken and we just leave it hanging on to fool tramps. This door never did have a lock."

No locks, I thought. Were these people afraid of hurting someone's feelings if they showed the indelicacy of locking a door?

"This has a lock now," I said. "A nice, shiny, fifty-cent padlock. And I'll bet my last dime, and the nickel I have to boot, that the Cad's in there."

"Unless it backed off without leaving tracks, it is," Eve said. "But why?"

"I'm going to find out," I answered. "Maybe we can get in this stall through mine. Find a loose wall board or something."

"You can get over the top of the wall," Eve said.

We went into the stall where my car stood. I patted its back end fondly. It wouldn't be much good to me for a little while yet, but it was nice to know it was still here.

I went around the side of the car and flashed the light on the tires. They were still inflated. I flashed it through the rolled-up window toward the dashboard.

Eve screamed. The sound rang wildly in my ears, echoing violently in the confines of the shed. I wanted to scream too. Instead I grabbed her and hung onto her, trying to squeeze the sobs from her into my chest.

"Easy," I said roughly. "Easy."

"Let's get out of here! Please, please, let's go!"

I took her out. I couldn't stand it myself. The sight of that body propped in my car, its hands on the steering wheel. A hideous, headless body!

XX.

We stood outside holding to each other, and both of us were trembling so much it didn't do any good.

"Jesus!" was all I could say. Just thinking of the sight, looming at us, caught as it had been by the hard spot of the flashlight.

Eve couldn't say anything. She held on to me and shuddered.

Finally she pushed me away and took a deep, sobbing breath. "Give me a cigarette, Tom. Oh Lord!"

"We'd better go and call Saarkinnen," I suggested thoughtlessly.

"Why?" She was calmer now. The hand holding the cigarette hardly trembled. I took a cigarette myself; I was too far gone to cope with a pipe.

"Dead men are his job," I said.

"It seems to me," she said in an odd, contemplative voice, "that that depends on the dead man."

"It's Prigwell," I said. "I don't see who else it could be."

"I don't either. Now all we need is the head." She dropped the cigarette in the snow and crushed out the spark with a sharp twist of her toe. "But if is—especially if it is, Tom—don't you see what a spot you're in?"

I hadn't seen, clearly. Now I did. And then I remembered the plan of action I had formulated in the house. In the shock it had completely escaped me.

"I know a better reason for keeping the body away from Saarkinnen," I said. "I'll tell you later. Right now—" They were hard words to say. They put so concretely what I knew we must do. "Right now we'll have to get rid of—of it."

Eve sounded as callous as a killer in a packing plant. "Dump it over the wall and into the Cadillac," she said.

"That's easy."

"Who?"

"You." Which explained her callousness.

"The idea is," I explained, "to keep it out of sight .
Completely. Forever."

"No corpse—no murder," she reflected. "Isn't that
slightly felonious?"

"Do you mind?"

"Hardly, darling." She laughed—with emphasis.

I took the flash, dropped the stub of my cigarette, and
went back into the garage. I was hoping Eve would come
with me. It wouldn't matter what she did; she could stand
and make remarks on all my antecedents for all of me. I
just wanted someone about while I was juggling the
corpse.

I turned to see if she were coming; she had
disappeared completely. I started to call, then thought,
she knows what she's doing, and hoping she really did, I
ducked into the garage.

Getting as far as the car door was easy. But trying to
open the door was another story. The door wasn't
locked—locking a canvas-topped car is wasted effort—but
the thought of what I was to meet held me back. *The
Legend of Sleepy Hollow* had once struck me as funny. It's
peculiar how quickly views can change. Now I was one
with Ichabod Crane, lacking only horses—and the head.

That was the first time I had thought definitely of the
head as such, and I didn't move while I let the whole
thought seep into my mind.

Unless we could find the head, our hiding the body
was pointless.

I took a long breath and jerked the door open. I
flashed the light into the car, trying to keep it and my
eyes off the body, looking on the floor and in the luggage
space, behind the seat. Perhaps—though I didn't have
any desire to meet a bodyless head—I would find it there.

I didn't have much chance to look. I felt something
press against my left shoulder. I put my hand up and met

something rough and soft. A suit coat. And then that demented body started slipping. I jumped aside and let it fall. Hell, it had no feeling and I did.

It slid sidewise and then went neck down off the seat and onto the floor of the shed, leaving the legs sticking up stiffly.

I moved—but fast. I wasn't going to push those legs aside just so I could see into the interior. I wanted no further acquaintance with that body. The legs weren't as bad as the headless trunk but they were far too much for me. My social leanings, slight as they were, were toward more animate objects. Natural animation, rather, not the sort this ghastly thing had just displayed.

I wasted no more time on a gartered leg. I went around the car and looked in from the other side. There was no sign of the head. I was about to back out of the garage altogether, leaving the corpse to the darkness and its solitude, when all hell broke loose in my eardrums.

I went into a crouch, pressing myself against the wall, trying to keep out of the way of the machine-gun bullets I felt sure were aimed for me. I didn't think in those few moments; I just reacted.

The noise went on, a terrifying, stuttering roar. I was sweating more than I had during my short bout with the body. And then I realized the cause of the God-awful noise. I started cursing furiously at myself for being such a chicken-livered idiot and at Eve for not warning me.

A moment later the roaring weakened as she backed her banshee of a car into the open. It wasn't so bad now that the noise wasn't reverberating wholly within the shed.

I heard her zip back until she was level with my end of the shed. She cut the motor until it was only a soft grumble.

"Tom!" Her voice was urgent.

I went outside, gladly.

Eve had the rumble seat open. "Where's the body?"

"The head," I said. "We need the head."

She came up to me. "Stop babbling. Why do we need the head?"

"Why hide a body and leave the head to be discovered?"

She said, "Of course. But let's get the damned body tucked in here first. I'll take the feet. Hurry; this car will attract the ghosts from here to Canada."

She should worry about that! She was going to take the feet and *tuck* the body into her car. I had always suspected women of being a lot tougher than men.

She practically pushed me back into the garage, and whether I liked it or not, I got that hideous, stiff thing by the armpits and lifted them level with the feet, now resting on the cushions.

Eve took the feet and, grunting slightly, we went out of the garage. I was leading, walking backward. I was trying to run.

"Not very heavy, is he?" Eve commented.

"Not heavy enough," I grunted. "I wish he was too heavy to lift."

"Step on it!" was the only satisfaction or reply I got. We reached the car and, under directions, I slid my end over the edge of the rumble seat and together we pushed so that the body went inside at an angle. The legs came up to the top of the seat cushion. If he had been much longer—with the head on—we couldn't have got the top down.

Eve slammed and locked the rumble. "Close the garage doors—and hurry!"

I hurried, but before I could reach the Moon I had to stop. The sweat was breaking out all over me, and it was icy where the frigid air hit and half froze it on my skin. I thought what a pity it was that I had to stop and give up the remains of Bossy's fine wedding supper.

After a moment I felt better and I made it to the car and collapsed on the seat. Eve started it with a jerk that spun mud and ice wildly from under our wheels and we went down the alley, skidded around the driveway, and headed for the street.

We didn't make it. We were as far as the back end of the hotel when our headlights picked up a big, familiar figure. It was Saarkinnen and he was waving his arms and yelling something we couldn't hear.

Eve couldn't drive on without hitting him. She said, "God-damned fool," jammed on the brakes, and threw the wheel hard to the left.

It was a beautiful manoeuver. If she had stopped and backed around, Saarkinnen would have had time to get to us and jump on the running board of the car. As it was, our rear end whipped to the right in a skid, and when we had made a half-turn Eve let off the brakes and rammed the throttle. We roared, jumped, and went back the way we had come.

And I was married to her! I foresaw a short but swift life for myself.

She didn't turn at the alley this time. At the other side of the alley from where the drive opened onto it was forest. It looked to me as if we were going square into the trees. But she seemed to know what she was doing.

"Hang on," she said. "An old logging road—bumpy."

I agreed, trying to keep from going through the top of the car. It was a very old road, and bumpy was a mild enough adjective. However, it didn't last long. We went perhaps an eighth of a mile, swung left for another quarter of a mile, and spilled out onto a gravelled secondary road.

There was plenty of snow here, but it was rutted and we stayed in the ruts and went along without skidding.

"How did you ever get through that logging road without chains?" I asked when I could talk again.

"When I was getting the car around to your shed," she said, "I noticed tracks. Someone had broken trail for us. Momentum did the rest. Give me a cigarette. What do you think of that?"

"Of what, a cigarette?" I lit one and passed it to her. She was driving easily and swiftly.

"No, of another having been over the logging road? Thinnish tracks. It isn't used much—never in the winter."

"Maybe Saarkinnen used it to sneak up on the hotel," I hazarded.

"No," she said, "a model T would be my guess. If you noticed, the tracks stopped and went off to the right shortly after we made the left turn."

"I didn't notice," I said bitterly, "because I had my eyes shut! All right, it was Dirkson. What does it prove?"

"Just this," she said cheerfully. "He drove into the woods and parked off the road. We heard his car grinding up but didn't hear it leave, nor did we locate it like we did the Cad. So that's why we didn't see it. It's probably still there, under the trees."

"And Dirkson," I said, "no doubt has been pussyfooting around all of this time. He may have heard us talking in the house and seen us shoving the body around."

I didn't like to think of it. My mind was too filled with heads, my own and the missing one—I hoped it ached as badly—to concentrate on anything else.

I said, "Eve, if Dirkson didn't see us, Saarkinnen will be in our hair."

"I couldn't very well stop and invite him along," she answered sarcastically.

"Hardly," I agreed. "We can tell him we were drunk and celebrating. He won't believe it but he can't prove otherwise."

"Not unless he follows us," she said.

"Could he?"

"He could," she said flatly. "All he has to do is stop and let his ears guide him."

"We could have taken my car."

"It's a very nice car," she said. "We'll use it to snub the neighbors. But for speed I'll take this." And to prove it she jammed harder on the throttle. The hills and forests picked up the roar of the exhaust and bounced it back at us.

I held on to my head, but it was Prigwell's I was thinking of. That and the cheerful thought that if Saarkinnen found us I was a gone goose; and if Dirkson had seen us, Eve and I were both in for it.

XXI.

There was a last jolt and suddenly Eve put on the brakes, cut the switch and lights, and we were stopped in the middle of nowhere.

At least it seemed nowhere to me. All around I could make out the blackness that would be the trees, and the snow distinguished itself by being the least bit lighter than the surrounding darkness.

Eve evidently knew where we were. She slipped out of the car and walked around to my side. "Take it easy, darling. We don't want to be heard."

"By whom?" I whispered.

"Morozzi's chickens," she said in a soft voice. "I think we threw Sarky off—until morning at least. He can follow our tracks then. I have a perfectly grand idea."

The moon came out again from behind the clouds and I looked into Eve's dancing eyes. The thrill of her idea had for the moment blotted out all of the horror of our undertaking. I was glad of it—for her. It would take a more hardened woman than Eve to stand much more of the same thing without a break.

I slipped out of the car. "Your idea and Morozzi's chickens go together, I suppose," I said.

Eve smiled like a pixie. "Listen, Tom. We dig up that soft dirt in the chicken house and see what's at the bottom of it. And then we put our corpse in there. If Sarky does find it—"

"Then Mrs. Morozzi gets the blame," I said.

"No," she objected. "Raymond does. At least I think he does. She evidently knows him, and Sarky will find that out."

"I'd rather the body could be put some place where there was no chance of Saarkinnen finding it—ever," I said.

Eve's face lost its grin and became sober and worried. "I know, Tom, but I wouldn't. I want this to—to come out into the open and get over with. I don't want to spend the rest of my life worrying about all of these things."

"We'll play it your way," I agreed. I didn't feel the way she did, although I could appreciate her point of view. It wasn't that I looked forward to living under a cloud of worry the rest of my life, but I just didn't trust the police. Eve might get in the clear by turning evidence and she might not. They didn't as a rule, go much for altruism.

Playing it her way involved my wrestling the body out of the rumble and sliding it onto the snow-covered ground. That wasn't as easy as getting it in had been. Time and the warmth from the closed seat had removed the last of rigor from Prigwell's body and he was loose and wobby in my hands. I was nearly fit for the sanitarium Anitra had claimed for me by the time I had him sliding off the fender and onto the snow.

"You take the shoulders and I'll take the feet," Eve said. "I'll go first." She held one foot in each hand and led the way as easily as if she had a path under her feet to guide her. I followed along with the rest of the body, trying to keep the grisly neck from touching me.

We broke out of the trees after about ten minutes. I was sweating heavily in spite of the cold, and weary from fighting snow. It wasn't a kind of walking I was accustomed to and I found it hard going. Eve stopped after a whispered warning, and I looked for Morozzi's house. All I could see was a gleam of light that spilled out from the front. The rear, nearest us, was totally dark. The moon helped us by pulling another cloud across its face, and Eve started forward again.

We moved very carefully into the chicken house and let the body down without a sound. My eyes were accustomed enough to the darkness to see the blotches that I knew were hens on the roosts.

"They're reds," Eve said very close to my ear. "If they

were leghorns we wouldn't have a chance. They'd be squawking by now." She commented violently on the habits of leghorns and after a moment turned away.

I stood still, not knowing what to do, and heard rather than saw her slide out of the chicken house and disappear. She was moving across the snow as silently as I believe it was possible to move, but the night was so deathly still that the softest sounds could be heard to some extent. I tried holding my breath to keep from waking the hens, but it made so much noise when I let it out that I stopped and breathed normally.

Inside of five minutes Eve was back. She pushed the handle of a shovel into my hand and steered me about four feet from where I stood. I moved warily, taking care not to trip over Prigwell.

"Here's the place," she whispered. "You can tell which is soft dirt by the way it feels under your shovel. Hurry, darling, I'm nervous."

She was nervous! "My doctor would love to see this," I commented bitterly.

"You can have a long rest when we're through," she promised. Too long, I thought, and not in a place of my own choosing. But I dug.

I dug until the sweat was sliding across my eyes and freezing on my cheeks, and until there was a pile of dirt that seemed higher than the chicken house alongside the hole. Every now and then a hen would have a bad dream or something and Eve would make me stop digging until it settled down again.

And then I struck something. I stopped. "I've run into it," I told her.

"See how big it is."

I probed with my shovel, scraping a little dirt here and there until I found the extent of it. When it dawned on me what I was doing I set the shovel down and collapsed on the pile of dirt. The labor and the realization of what I had found made me sick at my stomach.

Eve held my head and stroked my streaming

forehead. "Tom, darling, what is it? Damn it, Tom!"

"You can reach down and feel," I said heartlessly.

She did just that, and a moment later she was beside me, shaking and holding to me. "Another one," she said in a gasping whisper. "Who is it, Tom?"

"I'm afraid to guess," I said. "But it isn't very tall– not as tall as I am. And it's sort of wide."

Eve got up, took my flashlight, and went into the hole again. I was feeling well enough to stand now, and I moved around to watch her. Bending almost double to shield the light from the hens, she snapped the switch. In the brief instant before she turned it off both of us saw the face I had uncovered. I had only seen it once before but I knew.

"Mr. Morozzi never did get to Lewiston," I said to her.

She came up shivering. "Can you stand it long enough to—to lift him out, Tom."

"Lift him out? I'm going to shovel the dirt back," I whispered. "We'll take Prigwell somewhere else."

"I know," she answered, "but I want to see how he was killed and—well, if there isn't something else buried underneath him."

It seemed I had married a ghoul with a one-track mind. Eve had come to find what Morozzi's chicken house concealed and she was determined to carry it through. Or to have me carry it through. After all, I reasoned, a man has to be obliging on his wedding night.

It was plenty tough, but I wrestled a very stiff Mr. Morozzi from his heathenish grave and rolled him alongside Prigwell. Leaving Eve to find out how he had died, I started digging again.

She came up to me. "He was killed the same way as Prigwell. The back of his head was caved in."

"Spare me the grisly details," I said. "I've struck something else and I want the strength to dig it out."

She sat down on the pile of dirt and waited patiently for me to play around and finally haul up a square wooden box roughly two feet by two feet. "This is it," I said.

"We can't open it here," she protested. "Besides, I've had enough of this place. I'm getting the creeps."

Well, that was dandy. What did she think I was feeling? I was beyond words, and, rolling Morozzi's body back into the hole, I shovelled the dirt in as fast as my short wind and aching muscles would let me. We patted the ground until we thought we had it about as it had been before.

"Mrs. Morozzi never gets up early," Eve said. "The hens will have it all scratched over before she ever sees it. That's good enough."

I rested while she put the shovel back and returned; then, under her directions, I hoisted Prigwell to my shoulders in a fireman's carry. She took the box—it was surprisingly light—and we went as fast as we could back to the car.

I let Prigwell jackknife into the rumble this time and closed the door on him. Eve put the box in my lap as I fell into the seat of the car and then she got in and started off.

I was so done in I could hardly talk. Things were blurring before my eyes and weariness was shaking every muscle. I didn't feel better, even when Eve reached out a hand and patted me.

"You're sweet."

"So is Prigwell," I answered disgustedly. "I'm getting so fond of cuddling that corpse I'll hate to see it buried."

She ignored me and drove in blithe silence. She felt, I suppose, as though we had done a fine night's work. I couldn't even feel.

The car wound up in a small groove of trees before I was aware that we had gone much of any place. That shows how tired I was. We had come twelve good miles through snowy back roads and were right where we started, and still toting the corpse. I was half under the impression we had hardly left the chicken farm.

Eve had the brilliant idea, she told me as she cut the

motor, of putting the body where no one would ever think of looking for it. So there was nothing to do but haul it from the rumble seat again and start toward my little house. We got it to the edge of the little spur of trees that ran almost to the bedroom window when she set her end down.

"Rest a while, Tom; I want to see about a few things." I dropped my end of the body and once more went into my waiting game. It took her about ten minutes to return this time, and I had spent five of them sneaking to the rear of my house with the box we had uncovered.

She was quite cheerful. "Dirkson's car—or rather, Bart's—is gone and so is Sarky's," she announced. "We can carry it in the front way."

XXII.

I didn't argue but I was thinking. If she planned to have a headless corpse in the house she was going to be minus a husband. I wanted no bodies knocking about in my nuptial chambers.

I let her take the lead again and she brought me right around to my front porch and into the living room. After dropping her end of the body again, she switched on the light and went into the bedroom. That light went on and I heard her moving about. Then she came back and picked up Prigwell's feet again.

In to the top of the steps was as far as she went. From there on it was my job. "Because," Eve said with a smile, "it's easier that way."

I used the fireman's carry again and started down the steps. I was moving automatically now, too tired to fight back and refuse to do anything more. Besides, I knew that since we had got started, we couldn't stop. We were like the proverbial bull and the tail and we were stuck with it.

I got within three or four steps of the bottom before I missed my footing and fell. When I realized I was going forward I got my hands under Prigwell and gave him a push. The heavy thump was his landing, the lighter but more vehement one, mine.

This time I was through. I swore it as I picked myself up from the cold of the basement floor. Prigwell could lie there and stink us out before I'd lay another finger to his ghastly body. I left him where he had landed and marched back up the stairs.

I dropped onto the still unmade bed and tried to relax.

Eve came and sat beside me. I grabbed her arm and hauled her alongside me.

"Damn it," I said, "let's take a bath and get some rest. Let's try to act as if this was our wedding night."

"You confuse me," she retorted. "How can we and rest, too?"

She wriggled against me and kissed me once, lightly. "I'm sorry, darling, but we have so much to do."

"What?" I demanded. "What other crimes are there left?"

"Lots of things," she said, ignoring me. "First, we'll go drink coffee. Bossy made up a big pot. We'll need it to keep awake."

"She's up?"

"No. But she was awake when I went in. She started the coffee when she heard me drive off. She thought we'd be chilled."

"I am," I said. "And after we take time out and have midnight coffee, what will we do then?"

"Well, we want to get a look at the Cadillac, put my car away, hunt for that head—and just lots of things."

I didn't like the way she added that last. I followed her, trying to resign myself to the more active life. The peace and quiet of a small town! The easy, leisurely existence of a weekly newspaperman. Plenty of time and energy to devote to my writing!

"Just what are these 'lots of things'?" I asked again as we reached the front door.

"Oh, you know, things will turn up," she said.

I stopped and shut the door she had half opened. "Now wait up," I said. "I love you, Eve—despite all this. In fact, that I could have gone through it all and come out with no desire to lay you and everyone else here alongside Prigwell proves I must love you.

"But I'll be damned if I'll do anything else until I know what it is. And that's that."

She put her hands on my shoulders and rubbed herself against me like an ingratiating kitten. "You're sweet—I just thought we'd better go to Letsburg and see Anitra's hotel room."

"For what?"

"Look through her private papers and such."

"Do we knock her and Raymond what's-his-name on the head while we do it?"

"Raymond Parkman, darling. No, but did it ever occur to you that they might not be there? Their car is in our carriage shed. I don't think they walked back to Letsburg."

That didn't cheer me at all. If they weren't in Letsburg, where were they? Prowling about after us, or had they joined Joseph Prigwell in permanent exile?

It was snowing again as we got outside. Thick flakes that gave the promise of continuing a while. The light through the kitchen window of the hotel made a yellow square on the snow and it was warming and pleasant. We made directly for that warmth without pausing to argue on the way.

There was no one in the big kitchen. A slow fire was going in the range and until I stepped close to it and felt the heat of the room envelop me I didn't realize just how cold I was.

Eve poured the coffee into two thick mugs while I stood and absorbed the warmth. Then she dipped her hand into my pocket and captured the cigarettes. I took one myself on the feeble excuse that I had earned it by this night's maneuvers.

The coffee was hot and strong. It had been on the stove too long to be good. But we weren't after flavor and it did what it was supposed to.

I looked at Eve. "Do you think Mrs. Morozzi killed her husband?"

She shrugged vaguely. "I don't know, Tom. I've seen her in moods when I wouldn't put it past her. But—" She shook her head. She seemed more definite now. "No, I don't. She had him tied in a knot. He knew she philandered with everyone but the town moron and he didn't stop her. He was afraid of losing her."

"Some men are that way," I said. "Over the damnedest

women, too. But I wasn't giving her a simple motive like permanently stopping him from objecting to her having someone on the side. I was trying to connect her with Raymond."

"And Anitra," she added. "They're a team, don't forget that."

"Maybe the box has a hint," I suggested.

"The box! Tom, I forgot it." She look disgusted with herself.

"I'll get it," I said. "It's right at the rear of the house. I put it there when you were snooping for Saarkinen and Dirkson."

"Let me," she said. "You've done enough. It isn't heavy. I'll take it in the house and we can open it when we finish our coffee." She got up and went out faster than I could even imagine moving.

I was crushing out my cigarette when that eerie thumping I had heard on my first day in the hotel was repeated. The door near the big range came slowly open and old Adam hobbled in. He was ghostlier than ever. He wore a white flannel nightshirt and, actually, a tasselled sleeping cap. His set, sour, wrinkled face peered at me from under the cap. He didn't try to come beyond the door but beckoned to me with an imperatively crooked finger.

I went toward him. He stood in the doorway and looked anxiously toward the direction in which Eve had gone.

"I got something to tell you. Don't say nothin'—to anybody."

I nodded. "Shoot."

"No time now. Tomorrow. I'll be cutting wood. Come out and give me a hand. It's important."

"Will it keep?"

"Not for long." There was no expression on his face to hint at what he might mean. His sunken eyes stared almost blankly into space. "Make it early. Seven o'clock."

I groaned at that. I'll be there."

"You might bring a cigar," he said.

Insofar as it was capable, his face held an expression: hope and anticipation.

That was a relief. I had been planning to use Adam's love of cigars to good advantage. Now it seemed he was going to meet me halfway.

"I'll bring a handful," I promised.

Eve made sounds coming in, and Adam jerked and started hobbling across the room. She opened the door and stared at him. I saw a flicker of suspicion on her face. It disappeared, as he said, "Can't get through a whole night no more, Eve. Must be getting old." He went through the door, his pegleg thumping hollowly.

Eve eased the door shut. "What did he have to say?"

"Just what he told you," I lied. "He scared me half to death. That leg makes a funny sound."

I was wondering what Adam had to tell me and why Eve should be perturbed about it. She evidently hadn't told me all she knew—and there must be something she didn't want me to know.

The snow was still coming down thickly as we started back to my house. We went directly in. Eve had the box in the middle of the living room floor, and neatly arrayed on top of it were a claw hammer and a small crowbar.

"It's all yours, darling," she said magnanimously.

This was something I could do while sitting down, and I took advantage of it. It wasn't much of a job opening the box; the lid was nailed on and the corners covered with little tin caps. Getting those off and then the nails up to where I could get the hammer claw over them was less than five minutes' work. I tossed the lid aside and pulled at the sheet of heavy brown paper that lay just underneath it. Eve was beside me, breathing down the back of my neck.

"This proves something," she said, as I lifted the first of the thick cellophane envelopes from the box. That's all it contained, envelopes of cellophane, and inside each of them a pair of women's hose.

"It might prove that Mr. Morozzi was doing a little

digging on his own," I said. "And got caught finding this."

Eve was busy ripping open one of the envelopes. "They're silk, Tom." She held a pair of the hose up to the light and ran her fingertips lightly along them. "Really silk!"

"I've never seen a more avaricious look on anyone's face," I remarked.

"It's been a long time . . ." she murmured. She turned the hose about and looked at the tops and at the toes. She replaced them carefully in the envelope. "Japanese silk, darling," she said. "It proves a lot, doesn't it?"

"It's a mess we've damned well got to get you out of," I retorted. I got up. I didn't like the looks of this thing. Less now than ever. I wanted to get that box out of sight. My weariness was still with me, but I felt a new surge of energy to help me over the things I knew were yet to be done tonight.

"In the basement?" I asked.

She nodded absently. I turned from her and put the lid back on the box, nailing it lightly. Then I took the whole thing, paper, tin corners and all, to the cellar. I left them there with Prigwell and went back upstairs. Eve came up to me and took my hands. "I'm scared, darling," she said. "I'm scared as hell, Tom."

I kissed the vivid red mouth lightly. "There's plenty to do to keep your mind off it," I said. "Let's go."

"They're in pretty deep, aren't they?" she asked as if she hadn't heard me. "They can't afford to stop, now."

I saw what she meant and it sent little shivers running up and down my spine. I was too good at mental pictures for my own good, and I saw Prigwell and Morozzi, and I could see Eve and myself, too. It was an ugly picture. I said, "We can't afford to stop either. We'll have to stay one jump ahead of them."

Eve swung toward the door. "Ideas, Tom?"

"Lousy with them," I said. I didn't add that the ideas I had didn't reconcile with one another. I couldn't quite add Prigwell and Morozzi together. Even though they had been killed in the same way. I couldn't make the whole thing fit—and the pieces that were out of place just weren't the kind I could mention to Eve.

"Where to first?" I asked her.

"We might take a look at the Cadillac," she said. "I have some ideas too."

When we got to the garage her first idea seemed to be to have me shinny over the wall and drop into the next stall. I pointed out that I was hardly a high jumper and there was no room for pole vaulting.

"We can get a chair out of the house," she said. "That will do it."

"How do I get back?" I demanded. "Or do I spend the night waiting for Anitra and Raymond what's-his-name to come and let me out?"

"Parkman, darling. And when you get to the top of the wall I can hand the chair to you and you can drop it over the wall."

"I have a better idea," I countered. The less I wandered through that deepening snow in oxfords the better I would feel. "There's a box full of tools in the turtleback of the car. We can use that."

She agreed on that and I got out my car keys and unlocked the turtleback. It was a good deep one, extending all the way forward to the partition that was a short distance behind the seats. Ever optimistic about the performance of cars, I kept my tools shoved so far forward as I could and piled my luggage in after them. Now I had to clamber into the rear of the car and reach for the box.

I handed the light to Eve. "Hold it while I crawl in," I said. I got over the bumper and doubled my back and wormed my way in. "Shoot the light this way," I ordered. When she did I saw the box and reached for it. I pulled it over the floor toward me. A corner of the box caught on the fibre floor matting and the box stuck. I gave a hard yank to free it. The box, instead of coming free, tipped over frontward—and the hideous head of Prigwell rolled out and came directly for me.

I screamed. At least, Eve said later that I did. I wasn't responsible for my actions just then. I was jammed double in there, and when that head came at me I tried to back out and straighten up at the same time. My head hit the metal top of the turtleback cover and I was nearly knocked down on top of the gruesome thing.

I tried again, wishing frantically that I could curse and cry all at the same time. I went out like a terrified crab, hit the bumper as I cleared the car, and went sprawling onto the dirt floor. I lay there for a moment and retched.

God, what a horrible sight, the eyes still open, the face frozen in terror, the hair awry on top!

Eve gasped. I heard her do that. Then she was beside me, patting at me, moaning a little.

"Tom, are you hurt? What a hellish thing! Are you all right, Tom, darling?"

I'll love her forever because she didn't laugh at my pratt fall.

"I'm sick," I said. "I wish I could be clumsy enough to kill myself sometime."

Finally she managed to get me on my feet. She retrieved the flash from the dirt where she had dropped it when I tumbled. Now she turned it on the head.

"It is Prigwell," she said in a cool, detached way, as if she had a bug under a microscope and were examining it for irregularities. "So now we're sure whose body we have."

"Weren't we before?" I kept my eyes away from the back of the car.

"Reasonably sure," she admitted. "Well, I suppose we'd better put it with its body. It would be worse for Sarky to find this than the rest of the corpse."

Suddenly a thought struck me. "Hey," I said, "no one but myself has had the car keys. How could that head get into a locked turtleback?"

"It couldn't. No one?"

"That's it," I said. "No one but me and Saarkinnen."

XXIII.

I was getting tired of trying to hold myself on top of the beam which I had straddled painfully, so I said, "Hand me the box, darling."

While she was getting it up to me I glanced over the wall. Up to now I had looked only on my own side. I looked back at Eve. "Set it down," I said. "The Cad is gone."

"Gone!"

"That garage contains so many cubic feet of empty air," I told her. "And nothing else that I can see." I lowered myself by my hands until my feet found the box. I released my hands and managed to get to the ground without breaking my neck or the flashlight. I stood there, panting, and looked at her. "What do you think they were up to while we were out prowling?"

She touched the tip of her tongue to her lips. "If they followed us we couldn't have heard them—the Moon makes too much noise."

"And," I finished her thought, "if they saw us uncover Morozzi and they put him there!"

"Yes," Eve said. "I'd rather you didn't say it, Tom." She started toward the door. "I'm going to put the Moon away. Get your car backed out, will you?"

I waited until I heard the low, distant rumble of the Moon's exhaust and then backed my convertible into the alley and waited for her. I spent the time in trying to piece things together. There were two opposing theories. And the only conclusions I could reach were that one was half wrong or the other was all wrong. I would have preferred the latter, but down inside I felt that it wouldn't work out that way.

Eve garaged the Moon and I coasted the convertible

alongside her. She slipped in the driver's side, so I slid over and let her do the driving. I was relieved. She was a good driver and I was too tired to feel like coping with snowy roads. I lit a cigarette for her before she could ask for it, got out my pipe and tried to relax.

We turned into the driveway and headed for the main street. Our headlights picked up a Model T corning slowly toward the hotel.

"Dirkson?" Eve asked.

"Or Bart," I said. "Can you tell their cars apart?"

"No," she said. "Tom, it's following."

I glanced through the rear window. The weak yellow light from the T's headlamps was swinging around in an arc as the car made a U-turn. Eve jabbed at the throttle and the convertible gave a satisfying jerk and began to roll.

"Just what are you after at Anitra's?" I asked. "Besides, of course, the marriage paper."

"A mask," she said. "That's why I wanted to search the Cadillac. A mask and a fur-collared coat and a muffler. And probably a hat, too."

"Why?" It was a natural question, I thought. The thing didn't make sense to me.

"I'd rather not say," she answered. "I have an idea—only it's not in presentable shape yet." She patted my hand. "Mind?"

How could I? That made two of us with private theories. So I said, "No."

We parked in the dark, snow-covered lot behind the hotel. There was no sign of the Cad. I followed close behind Eve. She seemed well acquainted with the layout of the hotel, and instead of going to the front door we went in through a half-hidden rear entrance.

We were in a small corridor lighted only by a dim red light to indicate a fire exit. It branched some ten feet from the doorway through which we had entered. Eve took the right corridor. "The other," she whispered, "goes to the kitchen."

"And this one?"

"To the lobby, but we won't go that far. The night clerk knows me, and he's one of these wide awake people."

"In Letsburg?" I mocked.

Eve grunted. "Get used to it," she said.

About ten feet from a swinging door we turned and went up a flight of narrow stairs. On the second floor we followed the corridor to the top of the wide main stairway. "You take it from here," Eve said. "I don't know which room is hers."

I remembered the turning I had taken and we made it to Anitra's door. Eve smiled at me, dug into her mackinaw, and came up with a plain skeleton key. I started praying they were out. A reception party would be no fun right now.

"Never trust a small hotel's lock," she said. "Or a big one's, for that matter."

She bent, inserted the key; it turned easily, and the door was unlocked. "That's why you should always keep your key in the door when you're in the room," she said.

I opened the door and peered cautiously in. The room wasn't very dark. A bridge lamp was on low bulb. It stood in the far corner by the davenport. Eve peeped around me, nodded, and we slipped in. She locked the door behind us.

The first thing she did was to go to the closet and look in. She stepped out and went to the door across the room. It was the bath. There was another door connecting it to the next room. It was unlocked. Eve turned the knob.

"Raymond's room," she said.

"That interests me," I told her. "You take this one and I'll go in there." I went past her. We left the doors leading to the bath open. In Raymond what's-his-name's room the light was on also. They were low-wattage bulbs, but there was enough light to see fairly well.

I realized belatedly that when I had visited Anitra before and she had ostensibly gone to the bath, she had in reality come in here to ask Raymond's advice.

The room was the same as the other except for the fact that, being a man's, it wasn't quite so neat. First of all I went for the dresser. The drawers yielded absolutely nothing. From the look of the dresser the room might be uninhabited. I tried the closet. A suit hung in it. A nice plain oxford gray business suit. Evidently Raymond wasn't always cast in the role of chauffeur. I spotted a pair of hat boxes on the shelf and hauled them down.

In one was a snappy felt sports hat in deep gray. It was a good make, only slightly worn. Inside, the size read seven and one quarter. The other box also held a hat. I had half expected to find Burnham's Homburg, but this hat too was a sports model. It was a greenish number with a rakish feather in the band. But what interested me most of all was the size. It was six and one half, a damned small headsize. So Raymond wore two hats, six and one half, and seven and a quarter. Elastic sort of guy, I thought.

I took a second look at the suit. The pockets were completely empty, but there was a label stitched into the top of the inside coat pocket. And the suit was a thirty-four. I'm no tailor, but I knew without hesitation that Raymond was a hell of a lot bigger than that. I wore a thirty-eight myself, and he was huskier than I.

I went through the room, seeing nothing else of interest, while I thought it over. Eve came into the bathroom.

"Tom!" she said, after making a sharp metallic sound with something.

"Yeah?"

"What color is Anitra's hair? Yellow, isn't it?"

"More or less. Why?"

"And what would you say about Raymond's beard?"

"That would be blond or red, I suppose," I said. "Why ask me? You know them better than I do."

"I just wanted corroboration," she said. "I've found a

razor in here with black hairs on the blade."

I went in. She was right. It was a safety razor and whoever had used it had failed to clean the blade. The hairs were black. .

"Maybe Anitra's not a natural blonde," I suggested, "and used this on her legs."

"She's a blonde," Eve said. "She uses rinses, though. Anyway, she was one of those women who don't have hair on their legs—at least when I knew her."

She sounded envious. I patted her bottom. "Smart girl. This gives me ideas. Now if we can find another razor."

We did. But it was neatly wiped and told us nothing.

But I didn't want any more. I had enough now to play a hunch. I said to Eve, "Is the telegraph office open all night here? Better still, can I put a phone call through without every word being gossiped all over town?"

"Not unless I get on the board. The night operator's a friend of mine, but her tongue is loose at both ends."

"Could we hit her on the head and get rid of her?"

"Have you an idea, Tom?"

"I have, and it means a long-distance call to San Francisco."

She didn't ask questions. I liked that, because I wasn't sure enough of myself to answer any. And again a newspaperman's training kept me quiet. The story wasn't ready to break and I wasn't going to stick my neck out until I had my facts verified.

"All right," Eve said. "I can manage the telephone. Let's go."

"Find what you were looking for?"

She made a face at me; it was a cute face. "No mask. No anything. But I know there must be one. I'm sure it's somewhere. It has to be."

"Maybe it was buried out by Morozzi's chicken house and we should have dug it up along with the other loot."

"No," she said seriously, "it has to be somewhat handy." She looked startled and then chuckled. "Of course! I'm an awful idiot. Anitra has it with her." Then she shook her head. "But that doesn't explain the other things."

"What other things?"

"The overcoat and hat, darling. Unless they're in the Cad."

Which certainly enlightened me.

We started for the door leading from Anitra's room. That's all we did, start for it. Above the soft sounds made by our footsteps on the rug I heard a noise. I grabbed Eve by the arm, at the same time signaling her to keep still.

What I heard was a key being slipped very quietly into the door lock. Much too quietly for it to be the casual entry of the room's occupant.

We stepped against the wall so we would be behind the door when it opened. There was nothing to do but wait now.

The door opened suddenly as the lock clicked back. Whoever it was meant to surprise us—assuming he knew who it was in the room.

I caught the door as it bowled back toward me and when I saw a foot I slammed it back as hard as I could.

Eve and I shot into the doorway. I had one glimpse of Dirkson picking himself up from the overturned chair where he had landed and another glimpse of the key in the door—a key with a hotel tag hanging from it— before we barrelled into the hall and on toward the stairway.

Eve suddenly yelled, "Tom!" and Raymond drove at us from a corridor just off the main hallway. He had a gun in his hand but he wasn't shooting with it. He swung it at me like a club. I blocked the blow with my shoulder. It hurt like the devil.

"You sonofabitch!" I yelled, and kicked at him.

He had the advantage this time, and with his free hand he got me one over the eye. I took it pedalling backward, so it didn't hurt much. I kicked again and sent the gun out of his hand; then he moved in, limp and all, to slug it out with me.

That was all right with me. I was weak from a two-year stretch in a sanitarium and I was out of condition, but I had been in more than one Golden Gloves bout. The fact that I had always ended up on my fanny had only taught me what to watch for in the other fellow.

My real objection was that I didn't have the time to stay and make stew meat out of that pretty face. But as far as the law was concerned it was all on his side. I couldn't wait and have it out, not with Dirkson close by and Saarkinnen likely to show up at any minute.

I took his right with my forearm, tucked in my chin, and telegraphed a long, looping left. He ducked and I never delivered it. Instead I jabbed with my right and caught him as he moved, ducking square into the blow. It was the first time my favorite trick had ever worked for me.

I had the satisfaction of seeing him spill back and slap hard against the hallway wall, and then I turned to run.

Eve was still with me. Anitra had joined the party. But it was all Eve's show. She had the other woman's handsome fur coat jerked up her back and over her head. Eve gave a final hard heave on the coat down over Anitra's face, spun her around and delivered a neat kick in the tail with her heavy pacs.

Anitra went head first onto her face and we headed for the stairs. The whole thing had happened very fast because, as we went around the corner of the stairs, there was a loud yell.

"Our pal, Dirkson," I panted. "He finally got to the doorway."

"Was the shouting at them or at us?" Eve gasped.

I tripped over a step, recovered, and ran on. "Was he following them or were they trailing him?" I countered. "To hell with it now."

We got outside and into the car, and Eve was streaking it away from there before any of the three would have had a chance to do much.

I flopped. I was worn out and my chest hurt. "Now

what?"

"You want to make your phone call?"

"After that—more than ever. Fat chance now, though."

Eve was silent as she cut the car through the rough back streets of Letsburg. She turned onto the highway at the other end of town and came back down the main street as sedately as if we were the most innocent of people.

We passed the courthouse, but nothing seemed to be stirring in the basement section.

"We'll be so obvious we won't even be conspicuous," Eve said. She pulled to a stop before the lighted window of the telephone office, turned off the motor, and took the keys out of the car.

"Let's go in."

It was a minute office with but two booths. They were both for long distance. The local phones, three of them, were on a counter. The girl behind the board was chubby and dark with coffee-colored eyes the size of saucers.

"Eve! What are you doing out so late?"

"Things," Eve said. "Want to make ten dollars?"

"What do I do for it?" Saucer-eyes was all suspicion.

"Let me run the board for about five minutes."

"The last time I let someone do that I got caught. I can't, Eve."

"No one will know."

"Honest, honey—"

I wasn't doing so well at looking unconcerned. My head kept swivelling toward the doorway. We were in full view of the street; anyone could have seen us through the window.

"How much?" Eve asked insistently.

"It isn't that, Eve, honest." Her voice was high and irritating.

Eve played her ace. "I have two pair of nylons. They aren't new, but they're nylons and there aren't any runners in them. You can have your choice."

She was giving away her heart's blood and the chubby girl's integrity was sunk.

She let loose of her earpiece as if were hot metal. "I wish you'd take the board a minute, Eve. I've had to go for just hours." Eve set herself and the girl made for a door at the rear. It was marked "Private." She stopped and said, "Tomorrow—don't forget."

"Your props are as good as sheathed right now," Eve promised.

As the door closed behind Saucer-eyes she looked at me and grinned. "See, I do love you. Anyway, they aren't the same shade, those pairs, or I never would have let them go. Now get going."

I got. I angled into a booth and picked up the receiver. I gave Eve a name. "He'll be on the city desk at the *Mail* right now."

It didn't take long. The call went to the Coast and down, and finally I heard a familiar growl of a voice.

"This is Hallam," I said when we were connected. "I'll make a trade with you."

"Come home and write that column," he yelled. He was one of those people who talk in direct ratio to the distance of the opponent.

"No," I said. "I have to make this fast. Listen."

"You pinched?"

"Not yet," I said. "And I'm sober. I'll give you an exclusive on one of the hottest stories in this part of the country for some information."

"Give."

"You call me tomorrow—early—at the Hotel Vinson. Don't mention any names when you talk, either. I have control over this board now but I won't have tomorrow."

"For God's sake, give!"

I gave, plenty. And when I got through he said, "You're the same damned fool," and hung up. I knew I would get my information.

The regular operator was relieving Eve as I stepped out of the booth.

"Tomorrow," she reminded Eve.

Eve nodded. I said, "Charge the call to the Vinson Hotel-Mrs. Hallam."

"You louse," Eve said cheerfully. "It's all right," she added to the amazed girl. "I'm Mrs. Hallam." And we got out through a flood of questions and congratulatory squeals.

In the car Eve lit one of my cigarettes and blew a thoughtful smoke ring.

"I still don't see what you're after," she said.

"I don't either, for sure," I said. "I will tomorrow, though." I looked at the dashboard clock. It was four a.m.

"How about going home?"

Eve sighed. "It has been exciting, hasn't it?"

"Much too much."

She started the car. "We may be able to get some rest if Sarky doesn't wake us up too early."

I was looking at the courthouse while she talked, and I saw a car pull quietly away from the side. As it passed under a street lamp I recognized Saarkinnen's V-8.

"We won't have to wait until tomorrow," I said. "He— or his car—is on the prowl right now."

Eve took one look, got the car into gear, and nearly took the rear end out as she started off.

If for nothing else, Saarkinnen could have got us for speeding.

I looked back. There were headlights behind us, coming closer. I groaned. There went my chance of sleep, and of keeping my date with Adam.

The V-8 rocketed alongside. Eve cursed luridly, but she stopped. The V-8 did too. The door opened and a man got out and walked up to us.

It was Bart.

XXIV.

"Evening," he said conversationally.

"It's hardly evening," Eve pointed out. "Now what's the trouble?"

Bart's cow-like features looked more placid than ever. "Nothing," he said in a surprised fashion. "I hope."

Eve's voice took on a little edge of exasperation as though this were hardly the hour to be indulging in the county police's variety of humor.

"You didn't chase after us just to say hello," she said.

"Well, no," Bart admitted. "I got a message to deliver. Sarky called up—I'm on duty tonight—and said if I saw you to tell you something."

"Where is Sarky?"

"He went to Spokane," Bart said. "Took some stuff with him to the lab there."

Eve lit one of my cigarettes. I contented myself with my pipe; it was a far better article when patience was indicatcd. And it was beginning to look as if Bart were going to stand there until dawn. It was cold and a light snow was falling, but he seemed blissfully unaware of any discomfort. I suspected that he regarded this in the light of a neighborly chat, and he was going to enjoy it to the fullest.

Eve had evidently decided to play along with him. "What stuff?"

"Seems he found an overcoat and scarf and hat all crumpled up. That was just before you took off so fast in the Moon tonight." There was no animosity in his voice. He could have been describing an ordinary leave-taking as well as our precipitous dash.

"Sarky called to you, but I guess the Moon was making so much racket you couldn't hear." That fooled no one, including Bart. "You really ought to get a muffler on that car, Eve."

"He called to tell us about the coat and things?" Eve asked patiently.

"Yeah. They looked like there was blood on them. Not an awful lot, but some. Sarky took them to Spokane to find out."

"Where did he get them?" Eve persisted.

"In Hallam's car, just back of the seat. He was going after the camera and things to make pictures of the body." He sounded somewhat aggrieved. "Then you stole it and spoiled everything."

Eve said, "Oh!" It seemed to be all she could manage.

I thought, "Good God, what a country. They censor you politely for swiping what was evidently Exhibit A!"

"Sarky called me to tell you if I saw you to come in to the office in the morning. He won't have time to run out to your place. And he wants to know if you'll bring the body?"

"We'll be delighted," Eve said wearily. "But it didn't have any head to speak of."

"No," Bart said matter-of-factly, "that was gone. We couldn't locate it. If you happen to run across it, will you bring it too?"

"If we run across it," Eve repeated. "What time does Sarky want to see us?"

"About ten or so. Don't hurry. You bolt your breakfast and you won't feel good. He don't expect you to get up too early." I swear he almost smiled. He waved his hand and turned away.

Eve leaned out of the window. "Bart, there was a row of some kind at the hotel."

"I know," he called. "I phoned in while you were in the telephone office. A little while ago. It's all right. No one was bad hurt."

Suddenly I remembered something, and with a muttered word to Eve I jumped out of the car and hurried up to Bart. "Got a cigar?" I asked him.

He slapped his chest pocket. "Couple of campaign

cigars I cornered the last time our Congressman was through here—awful ones."

"Hell," I said gratefully, "I don't care if they're poison. Will you sell them to me?"

Bart grunted and took two powerful-looking stogies from his pocket. He put them to his nose and sniffed and then let me smell. They were as strong as they looked. "Take 'em," he said. "I only use 'em for Sarky when he runs out of plug."

"Thanks," I said. "I'll buy you some good ones."

"Never smoke 'em. Only my pipe." He paused and took it from his pocket. "A pipe is mighty comforting when a man wants—"

"I know," I said, and left abruptly. It wasn't good manners, I suppose, but I was cold and Bart appeared to be in a talkative vein. I climbed back into the car. "Borrowed a cigar," I explained to Eve. "Every once in a while I crave one."

"Periodic smoker," she said. By her voice I knew she didn't believe me. But she didn't comment further.

We watched Bart get into his car and drive off. I looked at Eve and started chuckling. Pretty soon I was laughing. I was in one of those tired moods where everything was horrible and at the same moment ludicrous. I couldn't stop laughing until I was on the verge of hysterics.

"Sorry," I gasped, when I had subsided. "I was just thinking of our being so obvious we weren't conspicuous, and of roaming madly around the countryside trying to hide Prigwell's body from Saarkinnen."

Eve's smile was wry. "I'm thinking of hauling that body to Letsburg, after all your efforts getting it into the cellar." She started the car and drove slowly toward home.

It wasn't so funny now, after thinking about wrestling with that body again. I said, "What do we do with the head?"

"Leave it," she answered. "Unless you want Sarky to

identify the body right away."

"I'd rather wait," I said. "Unless something breaks, and it will. From the way Bart sounded, though, Saarkinnen isn't much concerned."

"It depends on what theory he has by ten o'clock," Eve said. "He might decide to charge us both and clap us in jail."

"And he might decide to hang us," I said. "Or just let us go with a slap on the wrists for being naughty."

"You don't get away with as much as you think you do in this country," Eve said. "We may be a lot of things here in the tall timber, but we aren't suckers."

Thinking of Bart's slow-spoken but accurate statements about our supposedly hidden movements of the early morning, I had to agree with her. But I was used to cops who wring a confession out of criminals first and then go out to look for a crime. This lackadaisical-appearing method of detection was too new to me to be understandable.

I gave up and watched Eve drive.

Even with war time there weren't many hours left until daylight. It was nearly five when Eve tucked the car neatly into the garage. She stretched herself and smiled at me. "There doesn't seem much point in sleeping, does there?"

I thought of my seven o'clock date with Adam. "Hardly," I said. "But I am damned tired."

We got out of the car and into the alley. I shut the garage doors and we started for the house. The snow had stopped again, and here and there a star had broken through the clouds. There was a slight wind that was cold enough to give us a little tingle of life. Otherwise it was still and peaceful. Looking at the dark scene, with only splotches of light where some farmer was getting an early start, it was hard to realize that in this quiet valley violent murders had taken place and might again at any time.

Eve said, "I move we build up the fire and have some

sort of breakfast. Then we might feel a little more like thinking."

I agreed absolutely; I was still trying to think of some way of getting away at seven o'clock. I had no idea what Adam wanted to tell me, but I felt inside a strong sensation that in his words would lie the key to what I wanted to know. Not that I believed Adam capable of murder and decapitation, but he was about the hotel and grounds a lot and his eyes had the look of not missing much.

It could be a forlorn hope born of wishful thinking. I was willing to take a chance that it wasn't.

We passed the woodpile. "I'll grab an armload for the fire," I said. Getting the sticks in my arms, I went on, "There doesn't seem to be much more cut into stove

length. I can kill a little time getting my exercise."

Eve didn't seem surprised, probably because she didn't yet know my aversion to physical labor..

"We'll eat first," she said.

I felt better now, having provided myself with an excuse to see Adam. After the light was on I glanced around, half expecting to see something different from what we had left. But it was the same; no new visitors, no more corpses.

I tossed the wood into the box by the stove. "I'll make a bargain," I told Eve. "You get the meal and I'll expand an idea I have."

"The bride," she said, "prepares the wedding breakfast." She smiled, a trifle ruefully I thought.

I kissed her on the tip of her nose. "Maybe we'll make this marriage legal before long—and then I'll get the breakfast."

"Can you cook?"

"Like Rector," I lied boastfully.

"Good," she said firmly; "then I can sleep in the mornings."

On that doubtful pleasure I took out the flashlight and walked into the yard. I was heading for the privy. I didn't go in. Instead, I stopped and walked around it and then paced to the porch of the hotel and back again. Following that, I paced to the little house. Then I made a circuit of the house, and on the far side I bolted across the narrow strip of tree-lined space that was between it and the hotel.

I stopped and looked at my wristwatch. I knew I had consumed too much time between leaving the privy and getting to the hotel. But I had run only in one place.

I returned to the privy and went through the process again, this time leaving out my jaunt to the hotel porch and back to the privy.

I was trying to piece it together, to fit it into my theory. It was the one thing that wouldn't go in very neatly. Outside of that, I had everything nicely set. Motive, opportunity, strength—everything but this one small item.

I lit my pipe and stamped up and down to keep myself warm. If only, I thought, I could figure how Bossy could have got to the house from the hotel in time to swipe the body, then I could prove her the murderess.

That was the way I saw it, but it was hardly a thing I could discuss cold-bloodedly with Eve. I couldn't very well go to her and say, "Your life-long friend, Bossy, clubbed Prigwell to death because she thought it might get you out of the mess you're in. She set off the bomb to get us out of the place so she could steal the body and hide it from the police. That was after she discovered you wouldn't like it if I was made the fall guy and the murder pinned on me."

It left several things unexplained, admittedly—the decapitation and hiding of the body in my car, and the way the head had got into the turtleback, those among others. But it was to me by far the most feasible theory. I could hardly see Anitra and Raymond what's-his-name killing their own partner unless there had been a double-cross. And even then I couldn't quite see them doing it in a place so likely to become public and cause their exposure.

And if the Treasury man, Dirkson, had done it, then he had good reason and certainly wouldn't have hidden the crime. I knew I hadn't, and that left only Eve, Bossy, or Adam. I doubted Adam's ability and tended to believe Eve's denial of any knowledge.

Which again left Bossy. Only I couldn't reconcile her moving that vast bulk from the hotel to the privy, setting off the bomb, getting back to the hotel by way of the far side of the house, and then coming to the privy again a few moments after we arrived there.

Assuming that she could have managed the time element satisfactorily, where had she taken the body until she found time to get it to my car, decapitate it, put the body under the wheel, and—how in hell, I finished wearily, had the damned head found its way into the turtleback of my car?

I was about ready to give it up when the house door opened and I knew it was time to eat.

XXV.

My typewriter and papers had been set on the floor and my little typing table set up before the couch. On it Eve had set coffee, bacon and eggs, and doughnuts. A bit of breakfast! The good smell of the food hit me as I stepped into the warm room, and I discovered I was ravenously hungry despite such appetite-upsetting items as headless bodies and bodyless heads.

"Wonderful, and you are veritably an angel," I said.

But Eve wasn't listening. She sat down with a far-away expression. "I still think if I could find the mask we'd know something," she said darkly. "I'm going to ask Sarky to search Anitra for it."

I cut rapturously into a perfectly basted egg. "If I had known you could cook like this I'd have married you years ago," I informed her. "And about the murder—I have an idea I want to talk to you about before we see Saarkinnen."

She looked interested. "But getting the murder solved won't help me out of the spot I'm in," she said.

"It might make it all the worse," I admitted. "The only hope is to try to blow this thing up so that your part doesn't enter into it."

"A sort of turning State's evidence?"

"No. Not unless you want Saarkinnen to know the details."

"I don't," she said miserably. "But with Dirkson here, I don't see how we can keep it quiet."

"That's something we'll find out," I said. It sounded cryptic, thinking it over, but I left it that way. I wanted to get to this other matter.

"About the murder!" Eve urged. She cut into an egg and poured ketchup on it. I shuddered.

But it made it easier for me, seeing her eat. I gave her my theory, as carefully as I could. She listened mutely, not looking at me, eating slowly and methodically. When I stopped she laid down her fork and sighed.

"It sounds like it could be right," she said. Her voice was low, toneless. "Just the thought of it makes me feel rotten, dirty inside. But—" she looked at me then—"I'm not enough of a coward to deny it, Tom. It's logical all the way through."

She was taking it, and I admired her for it. Not calloused, just steady, without hysterical denials she knew would be false.

"The only thing that doesn't fit," I reminded her, "is the impossibility of Bossy's getting to so many places at one time."

"And a reason for decapitating the body isn't very clear," Eve said in a troubled voice.

"To prevent recognition," I pointed out. "Only—how did she ever get the head into the turtleback?"

"You might ask her," Eve said with a mirthless grin. "But I wouldn't advise it."

She fell silent, absorbed in the new problem added to her others. I went on eating, feeling like an eel but still hungry, and it wasn't until we were on the final cup of coffee that she spoke again.

She poured the coffee and lit a cigarette in a preoccupied manner. "Tom," she said. She waited until I looked at her. In her tone there was something soft and pleading, yet imperative.

"What is it! Something you haven't told me?"

She nodded slowly. "It's about Bossy, Tom. I wasn't going to say anything, but I can see it's silly now—Sarky knows about the body. We can't hide that any longer. He might as well know all we have to offer. I—I guess I want to get this cleared up now no matter what happens."

She took a full breath and went on: "I saw Bossy just about the time that bomb went off. Just afterward, of course. You know how quickly we got outside! But I was behind you."

"She knows you saw her?"

"I don't think so," Eve said. "No, I'm quite sure she didn't. She was at the corner of the house. Hiding there until we got far enough down the path so she could—I suppose—bolt inside."

"That's impossible," I said. "She couldn't get from the privy to the far side of the house in the time between the bomb explosion and my arrival outside."

"I really saw her," Eve said. "Just a glimpse, but it was enough. It was Bossy—I know it." She looked squarely at me. "And I saw her before, too—while you were in Letsburg."

"Saw her? Here?"

"Coming out of here, Tom." Her voice was definite. She was obviously speaking against her will, yet it was something she could not help doing.

"I was coming back from the office and I swung along the veranda instead of going in through the hotel. My idea was to come here and see if you were comfortable. But when I got to the end of the porch, I saw Bossy coming out of your door. It was dark by then and it was hard to see. But I know Bossy well, in daylight or darkness. She sort of hesitated, as if she were looking around to see if anyone were watching her, and then she hurried into the hotel."

"You're sure it wasn't just someone else big," I asked. "Burnham, maybe?"

Eve smiled and squeezed my hand. "I'm sure it wasn't Burnham," she said. "Thanks for trying to help, dear."

A sudden, violent buzzing sound coming from the direction of the stove blasted into my ears so loudly that I nearly spilled my coffee.

"Telephone!" Eve said. She looked at the expression on my face and had to laugh. "You're wanted on the phone in the hotel, darling. I never did tell you about that little gadget, did I?"

"It sounded like an infernal machine," I said

apologetically. "That must be my long-distance call."

I got off the couch and headed out the door. If this happened to be the call I wanted, then some things— quite a number of them—would probably be cleared up. On the other hand, it might make matters worse. I couldn't be sure about that.

Bossy was starting breakfast for herself and Adam when I raced in. She didn't smile at me. She hardly seemed interested in my appearance.

"Long distance," she said in that abrupt way of hers.

"Thanks." I took the phone, wishing I had a little more privacy. "Hallam talking," I said.

After that I listened. I didn't have to ask any questions; they were all pretty well answered for me. At the end I said, "I'll get you the story as soon as it breaks. Take the toll on this call out of what I get—and thanks." I hung up.

Adam was stumping through the doorway buttoning a mackinaw around his throat. "Wood," he said to Bossy. "Call loud when breakfast's ready. I'm hungry."

He stumped out. I followed, went past him with only a brief "Morning," and went in to Eve. I put my gloves and coat on. "I'm going to cut wood with Adam. With him there I won't be so likely to cut my leg off."

"Your call Tom?"

"It was the one," I said. "But I don't know yet what it means. When I get through—" I went out.

It was still darkish at that hour and Adam had dug up a kerosene lantern from somewhere and had it sitting near the chopping block. He brought a heavy, double-bitted axe down on a thick chunk of pine. I watched the metal blade slice the pine in two and bite deeply into the chopping block. Adam worked it loose with a professional twist.

When I came up to him, he said, "See how easy that was?"

I admitted I was impressed.

"I don't want this told to anybody or I'd told it myself,"

he said cryptically. "What I'm going to say is between us. I'm tryin' to help, that's all."

"All right," I said. I gave him one of the foul cigars. He took it avidly and hid it in the depths of the mackinaw.

Then he put another log on the block and let fly with the axe.

"Remember what I said," he told me.

I didn't need any pictures drawn for it to sink in. I told him so.

"It's this," Adam said. He didn't stop working while he talked. I put the wood on the chopping block and he hit a crack. I put another piece on and he hit that. Sometimes he would stop and adjust the wood to get the grain in just the right place. He talked in spurts, between blows with the axe.

"Bossy took the body out of the house. She went in to check up on you. Bossy says by a man's things she can tell if he's fit for our Eve. She found the body. Then I saw Eve coming from the office and I rang the telephone bell so she could get out because she didn't want Eve to find her there. Otherwise, she would have taken it right then.

"She took it later. We fixed the bomb out of some old Fourth-of-July stuff and pried the privy loose from its foundations. I propped it with a stick against the far side. I tied a rope to the stick. When the bomb went off, I hauled oh the rope and pulled the board away and the privy went over. As soon as I got the board and rope pulled up to the porch, and hid, I came out. Bossy was already waiting by your house. When you and Eve came out, she went in and dropped the body out of the bedroom window. She would have hid it good then, but that big car came up and she had to get back to come out of the hotel like she'd been there all the time."

"She see who was in the big car?"

"No, just a man, that's all she knew."

"She didn't get the clothes?"

"Just the overcoat, scarf, and hat. Later she got the body and things and hid them in your car. She cut the head off and hid it in the back part. She would have cut the body up and hid it there, too, only when she was doing it someone pushed that big car in the next garage and she had to set still until they left."

"They? Did she hear what was said?"

"Sure. There was two of them. One, a man, said, 'We have to leave this here for a while. It's too conspicuous to hide in Letsburg.' That's as near as Bossy could remember it. Then a woman, that woman who says she's your wife, said, 'These local yokels will never spot it here.' And then they left. Bossy thought she heard someone else coming and she dropped everything and ran. That was Sarky."

"She wrapped the coat around the body when she cut off the head?"

"She used this axe and the coat to stop the blood. Wasn't hardly any blood, he was so dead and stiff-like."

I felt a little sick. I said, "How did she get the head into the back of the car?"

"That piece that separates the back place from the front of the car is two fiberboard panels. She unscrewed the clips that hold the one back of the driver's seat and pulled it loose. Then she put the head in the box."

So that was it! My theft-proof turtleback was no better than anything else a screwdriver would take care of!

Bossy stepped to the porch and bellowed: "Breakfast!

"And there's a phone call in here."

That was for me, I knew. I left Adam to hobble on in and went to the kitchen. It was Saarkinnen.

"Hallam? You and Eve better come early. Don't wait for ten o'clock."

"The Federal men get here from Seattle?" I asked.

"They's flying in." He didn't sound surprised that I knew they were coming.

"We'll be right in," I told him.

"Don't forget to bring a few things with you," he reminded me.

"I'll round the things up," I said. "And you'd better do

a little rounding up on your own hook."

"We are," he said.

That was that, I thought as I hung up. The Federal men were coming and Adam and Bossy's endeavors were of no use. Eve was on the spot—really on it.

XXVI.

I went in the house and told her of the message from Saarkinnen. I said, "I hope we can keep you out of it, but I don't know."

Eve had cleaned up the place and was sitting disconsolately on the couch. She looked at me and nodded with no apparent perturbation.

"I'd rather get it over with," she said levelly. "It was a good fight, Tom."

I ruffled her hair and kissed her. "You'll make a fine wife, Eve, and maybe I'll get a chance yet to find out."

"When I'm old and gray?"

"I'll be old and gray," I said, "if I have to lug this beastly corpse around much longer. Also bent. Well, let's get at it."

It was a much more unpleasant task than before. Hauling Prigwell, if it was Prigwell, about was a job that didn't get easier with practice. God knows I was getting plenty of that. Eve followed me with that hideous head.

Outside, I said, "We'll take the box of hose, too."

"Yes-but why?"

"Just on the chance that it might help." I went back for it. When I returned Eve had the Moon warming up. I raised my eyebrows.

She said, "You take your car. I'll feel better if we have the Moon too."

We did it that way. The head and body rode in the rear of my car. Eve followed me in, the Moon held at a discreet bellow.

Letsburg looked raw and desolate in the gray of early morning. There was little activity. Even at the courthouse nothing seemed to be stirring. I saw Saarkinnen's car parked in the rear alley, also two identical Model T's and an unfamiliar state police car. It had, I learned later, taken Saarkinnen to Spokane and brought him back.

I parked on the side street. Eve pulled up ahead of me. I got out and went over to her. She smiled thinly at me. "If they try to rope me in as an accessory, I'm running, Tom," she said. "I'm parked so I can go in a hurry, and this Moon will outrun anything in the State."

"They'll only make it tougher for you," I protested.

She reached under the dashboard and unsnapped a little automatic from a clip there. She showed it to me and then dropped it into her pocket. The action was grim.

"I've carried this for years. I've never shot it, but I know how."

I tried to be funny, without much success. "From the local wolves?"

"When I'm out at night," she explained. "It makes me feel better to have it."

"I hope you don't have to use it," I said fervently. I had more to say, but I heard footsteps. Turning, I saw Saarkinnen with a tall, spare man in the uniform of a State trooper. He nodded wordlessly to us and then introduced the trooper as Bowen.

"The Federal men aren't here yet," Saarkinnen said. "Where's Prigwell?"

"In the turtleback," I told him. "Is this just a routine questioning?"

"Among other things," Saarkinnen answered.

I pulled out my prize idea. "There's something I'd like to show you, Sheriff. Any objections to holding your questioning some place else?"

Saarkinnen's pale eyes were humorless but his lips smiled. "Morozzi's maybe?"

"We don't seem to be able to do much of anything quietly," Eve remarked.

"Not with that Moon, Eve," Saarkinnen said, and this time his eyes smiled too. "That might be a good idea, Hallam." He shifted a bulge in his right cheek over to the left one and spit tobacco juice on the snow. "I'll get a message to Bart and Mart and we'll follow you."

He didn't tell us why, but turned on his heel and strode back to his office. The trooper went silently to the State Police car and got behind the wheel. Eve started her motor and, after a nod from her, I went to my own car. Saarkinnen came out again and climbed into the police car and we started off. The Moon went first, but before we made a left turn on the edge of town she dropped behind. She parked carefully in Morozzi's driveway so that she had a clear shot at getting out. I wondered if Saarkinnen noticed it. But when he joined us at my car he didn't comment on it. Not that that meant anything.

"Get Mrs. Morozzi outside, will you?" I asked him. "There's something I want to do."

Saarkinnen looked levelly at me. "You want to play this hand, Hallam?"

"I want to play all of my cards first," I told him.

He looked from Eve to me and then at Morozzi's chicken house. "You'll need the break, I suppose." He said it softly, half to himself.

I didn't answer, and after a moment he and the trooper went onto the porch. Mrs. Morozzi answered their knock and they ducked inside. From our position in the drive Eve and I could see them reappear at the back, and then an arbor cut them from our view. Mrs. Morozzi was with them.

"All right," I said to Eve. "Let's hurry it."

She seemed to know just what to do. We got the body and the head from the convertible and carried them into Morozzi's living room. We must have seemed a strange sight to anyone who might have been watching. I lugging a headless corpse and Eve following with its head.

I set the body in a straight-backed chair, one with arms, and took the head from Eve. I placed it as neatly as possible on the grisly stump of neck. Then I laid Prigwell's hands on the chair arms. "All right?" I asked Eve.

"It's sickening—ghastly," she shuddered.

"That's what I want," I said. I started through the house.

We found them at the gate to the chicken house. Mrs. Morozzi stared sullenly at us. There was none of the moist-lipped, heavy-eyed warmth about her now. She was frightened and throwing up a defense of anger to cover it.

"I'd like to know the meaning of this," she said.

"We want to do a little excavating," I told her.

Saarkinnen silently handed me a shovel. It was the same shovel I had used before. I assumed he had picked it up on his way from the house. That didn't matter. But I hated the thought of using it. I gave it to the trooper.

"It's someone else's turn," I said, trying to smile. He grinned faintly, and stayed as silent as ever. I opened the door to the chicken house and led the way to the spot we had dug the night before. The chickens had scratched over the soft dirt as Eve had predicted, but it was still plainly the place to dig.

Mrs. Morozzi was as silent as the rest of us. Only her heavy breathing was obvious above ours. She moved away from us and leaned against a four-by-four for support. Saarkinnen shifted his position so that he was between her and the door.

It took the trooper far less time than I had taken to uncover Morozzi. I felt a strong surge of relief when I saw the poor devil come into view. I had been afraid someone had beat us to him. I heard Saarkinnen let out his breath.

Mrs. Morozzi screamed. She ran forward and dropped to her knees. "John!"

Saarkinnen looked at me. I said, "I was here yesterday and mentioned our blond friend Raymond to her. She knows him. She knows about this."

She swivelled her head. "I don't—I didn't! John!" She screamed it. But the acting wasn't good enough. There was too much of it, and Saarkinnen, who knew her, thought it obvious. I could tell by the look on his flat face.

He said evenly, "You're cutting up a lot more'n you would have when he was alive. You didn't think so much of him then."

"I did! I loved him. . . ."

Saarkinnen stepped forward and lifted her away from the hole so that the trooper could go on digging. She didn't resist him. She stood and shook and the sweat ran from her forehead down her face.

"You found this last night?" Saarkinnen asked me.

Eve answered. "Yes," she said. "Late last night. And something else."

"It's in the car," I said. "What Dirkson was digging for when you arrested him."

"You think Morozzi decided to do a little digging later?" Saarkinnen asked.

"And got caught at it," I finished.

"By Anitra?"

"Or Raymond or Dirkson," I answered. "Or Mrs. Morozzi, and she told one of them."

"Dirkson's been hanging around here," Saarkinnen said to no one in particular.

"How about that story of his busting out of jail?" I asked him. "Was it on the level?"

Sarakinnen's smile was brief. "No, that was to keep you guessing. He wanted it that way. He identified himself as soon as you and Morozzi left."

"And then he left?"

"In Bart's T," Saarkinnen said.

"He could have got to my place while I was shopping," I said. "In time to kill Prigwell."

"He could," Saarkinnen said. "But why should he— and not tell us?"

"Are you sure of his identification?"

Saarkinnen shrugged. "I wired Seattle. The description fits."

"When you get a look at Prigwell, I said, "you'll see the same general features. They look—looked alike."

Saarkinnen spit his plug out and wiped his mouth with a handkerchief. "That may be, Hallam. I wouldn't bank on it."

Eve started to say something; then she stiffened up. "The Cadillac," she said. "And Bart's T."

A moment later we all heard the two motors. Saarkinnen looked at the trooper still digging. "Let it ride for now," he said. "In the house?"

The question was addressed to me. I nodded.

Once outside the chicken house, we could see the Cadillac parked in the driveway and the T drawn up behind it. Bart was driving the Cad. Mart was outside. When he saw us he opened the rear door. He had a double-barrelled shotgun in his hand and he waved it a couple of times. Anitra and Raymond crawled out reluctantly. Dirkson came out of the T and joined them. Saarkinnen waved them toward the house and then we were in front of the arbor and out of their sight. We went into the house by the rear. I went ahead because I wanted to see how they were going to take Prigwell.

I got to the living room first. An instant later Bart herded Anitra and Raymond into the room, followed closely by Dirkson. He was still wearing the turtle-neck sweater and dirty slacks. He grinned faintly at me, and then when he saw the body his mouth went tight. Anitra stood just inside the doorway with one hand pressed against her breast. Bart had to push her aside to get Raymond what's-his-name into the room.

From behind me Mrs. Morozzi's scream sirened through the room. I swung around. She was staring wide-eyed at Prigwell. Saarkinnen took her arm and without a word she let him lead her to a chair. She collapsed into it and looked straight ahead of her. She was shuddering in spasms and the sweat was running in little rivulets down her cheeks. She would break, I thought.

Anitra had recovered herself, and she strolled to the couch and sat down. Raymond followed her and looked contemptuously around. He seemed totally unaffected by the body. The only one missing was Mart, or maybe Bart, and a moment later I heard the T start up. He evidently had gone back to town. For the Federal men, I presumed.

Everyone sat down but me. Saarkinnen gave me a nod to go ahead. I looked at Anitra. "You want to start?"

"Start what?" she demanded. Her voice had taken on a touch of shrillness. "What are you trying to frame? You won't get away with it," she informed us viciously. "I'll kick your dirty little police force from here to Seattle!"

"Now," Saarkinnen said mildly, "who won't get away with what?"

"For one thing," I said, "Anitra won't get away with suing me for bigamy. I had some interesting news this morning. She's Mrs. Raymond what's-his-name."

"Parkman, darling," Eve said quietly.

"Parkman," I repeated. "And she has been for quite a while. It's on the Seatttle records if anyone wants to check up."

"So what?" Anitra sneered.

"So," I said, "recognize our newest addition?" I jerked my head at the corpse.

For answer Anitra looked at Eve. "Of course you do, darling?" Her voice was heavy with suggestion. But Eve was either through hiding or still running a bluff. She just smiled back and shook her head.

I stepped in and let loose before Anitra could start spilling about Eve. I said, "There's one missing, Saarkinnen. There were five. One of them's dead—there in the chair. Three of them are in this room. Where's the other?"

"There isn't any other," Eve interjected quickly. And before Anitra could check her, Eve made a grab and got the other woman's purse. She unsnapped it and turned it upside down.

XXVII,

Anitra screamed, "Damn you. . . ." Saarkinnen got up and pushed her back.

Eve pawed the litter of junk from the purse and came up with a piece of rubber. She unrolled it. "A mask," she said. "The coat and scarf and hat you'll probably find under the back seat of the Cadillac."

Her damned mask! She had been so insistent on it. She was talking again. "I saw it in a college play years ago—so did Anitra." I saw Dirkson glance thoughtfully at her. Eve went on quickly, "Blow it up—it inflates— and hide the rest under a big overcoat, a muffler, and pull a hat down low and you have Ralph Burnham. She is Burnham."

I could see it now: how Burnham had on occasion been the only occupant of the car and yet out of nowhere Anitra seemed to turn up; and why he was always sleeping and not to be disturbed. The time Raymond had been in my house and Burnham had been in the car and yet Anitra had been the one to drive it away. It made sense.

"What the hell?" Anitra asked boldly.

"Is it illegal?" Raymond put in. "Is that what you pulled us up here to prove?" His voice was a cultured sneer.

"It only proves," I said, "that you have a remarkable front. And that there's something going on or you wouldn't bother with it.

"It fits in with a few things I want to tell," I added. I paused to let Anitra and Raymond do a little worrying. The rest of them were silent. Dirkson was lounging in a chair, his eyes constantly on my face. I wasn't quite sure yet how to fit him into the picture, but I had an idea and I was going to see how it turned out.

So I started talking. I sketched in a lot that everyone knew. I told of the smuggling.

I went on, "I was asked to come here and go to work for the *Vinson Record*. About that time Anitra and Company decided to move in here and use this as a nice quiet spot to distribute from. They figured the natives were so deep in their timber they wouldn't even know what was going on. But even so they were careful. They had their ears to the ground and they got wind I was coming." I paused for breath. It was circumspect. So far I had kept Eve pretty well out of it. The way I had to tell it would leave a lot of gaps, but I was going to try making it sound as if she weren't in it at all.

1 said, "They weren't the kind to kill except as a last resort. So they decided to scare me off one way or another. Not because I was anyone who had come in to oppose their racket, but because I was an alien, and experienced in noticing out-of-the-way things. Noticing them and writing of them is part of my business. I would be more likely to spot something, they reasoned, than the natives.

"So they worked up the marriage certificate racket. And had the nerve to get it to me through Saarkinnen, figuring the pressure from two sides would be enough to make me check out. Only they failed to take into consideration that I wouldn't bluff easily about having been married while so drunk I couldn't remember it. I wasn't that heavy a drinker and I knew it. They didn't. They also forget that at the time of the supposed marriage California had a three-day gin marriage law.

"But before that they tried planting stolen clothes in the house and hinting they were found by Government men so I could be scared off as an accessory. Only a corpse got mixed up in it and the whole thing blew up."

"No," Dirkson broken in suddenly, "they put the clothes there for two purposes. To scare you off or to increase the appearance of your being married to Anitra.

Whichever happened to fit into the scheme best. The old silk hose, you remember them, were a good touch."

"You were there when the stuff was planted," I said.

"And maybe swinging a length of stovewood when this—" I nodded at the corpse—"showed you up."

He grinned thinly. "I'll do my talking later. I was there, yes, and talking to 'this,' as you call it. But I assure you he was alive when I left."

"When you left?"

"Seeing those clothes was evidence against you and no one else, Hallam," he said. "They were technically in your possession at the time. I was giving the gang a little more rope. I left because the Cadillac drove up. The odds were too much against me—and I hadn't enough evidence. So I skinned out."

"And," I said, "Anitra and Raymond what's-his-name put two and two together and figured Prigwell was selling out to you. So they solved the problem."

"That's a lie," Anitra screamed. "He was dead when we went in there! Damned dead."

"They didn't go in right away that I noticed," Dirkson said. "I was watching."

"Not closely enough," I said stubbornly. "They went in ..." I was about to add, "before Bossy and Eve were there," but I checked myself in time. I wasn't making much sense at the moment. I still couldn't check it out whether Dirkson was himself or the dead man was Dirkson. I let it go like I had it.

"Then," I continued, "Mr. Morozzi started cluttering up the picture. He pulled a boner by yelling for the sheriff when he caught Dirkson digging in his chicken house. Or a boner from Dirkson's point of view. And after Morozzi got home he started thinking it over. Maybe he spotted Raymond or Anitra coming in to see his wife. Raymond most likely—Anitra wouldn't interest her. And he started doing a little digging himself.

"And," I said pointedly, "notice the similarity between the two deaths. They say a murderer repeats the method of his crime. Both men were killed by being beaten on the back of the head."

I turned, stepping close to the corpse and looking directly at Mrs. Morozzi. "Isn't that true," I shouted at her. "Isn't it true that one of these two caught your husband digging up that box of stockings they had there—*that they had there as a plant on you to keep you in line*—and that one of them killed him by beating the back of his head in?"

She looked up at me and shuddered. Her head shook violently. But she didn't make a sound. I said, "She'll turn evidence, Saarkinnen, or be executed with them."

I turned on her again. "Isn't that true?" And then I made a grab for Prigwell's head. I jerked it right off his shoulders and tossed it into her lap.

She let out a scream that will haunt me forever. A piercing shriek that ripped at our eardrums. She jerked upright and the head rolled on the floor. She screamed again and fell sideways. "She did it," she squalled. She pointed at Anitra. "I saw her—she did it!" And she scrambled on her hands and knees away from the head.

Anitra cursed filthily and got off the couch and rammed herself into Bart in one wild movement. Raymond followed her, and when she hit Bart, who had been standing placidly with the double-barreled shotgun, Raymond grabbed the gun as Bart stumbled.

He swung it on us. Saarkinnen had his gun half out of its holster and that's as far as it got. Anitra jerked open the door and raced for the Cadillac. We heard the motor roar over the sound of Mrs. Morozzi's sobbing and scrambling, and then Raymond backed out, leaped to the moving car, and it roared away

XXVIII,

Eve waited until they had gained the road and then she headed for the door. I followed her and managed to scramble over the side of the Moon as she sent it forward. I had a glimpse of Saarkinnen and the others tumbling into the V-8, and then we were moving too fast for me to do more than hang on .

The Cad was a good quarter of a mile ahead and going down the snow-covered side road like a dog with a firecracker on its tail. But Eve didn't have a hopped-up car for nothing. She laid the throttle on the floor and I gripped the door and prayed.

The Cadillac swung into a smaller road and Eve followed without slowing down. They came to a crossroads. She got her little automatic into her left hand, leaned out and shot twice.

"I told you I knew how to use it," she said. The words jolted out of her like hard, cold stones.

I didn't need to be told. The first shot took the Cadillac in the trunk and the second one caught what she was aiming at—the rear tire. The big car slewed crazily in the snow and then Eve squeezed an extra ounce of power out of the Moon and swerved it so that when the Cad stopped skidding by slamming sideways into a tree she was facing it.

I could see it as if it were slow motion. Raymond went up with the crash and hit the windshield. The shotgun roared over the sound of the car hitting the tree. Anitra got out and started running. Eve raised her gun and shot her between the eyes. Anitra went forward a short distance, carried by momentum, and then spilled in the snow. She was still half facing us. Eve laid her head weakly on the side of the car and was sick. Her little gun dropped onto the running board.

I jumped out and ran to the Cadillac. Raymond was a mess. The shotgun had jolted against him with the crash and when it went off it had been pressing against his side. There wasn't much left to his middle.

I clawed in the glove compartment of the Cad and found what I was looking for. It was a .38. I ran back to Anitra and put the gun in her hand. I pointed it at the hood of the Moon and pressed her finger against the trigger. The sound blended with the light snarl of the V-8's motor.

I got up and ran to Eve. "You shot her in self-defense," I panted. "She shot first—at least she shot. Raymond won't say anything. He can't. If Mrs. Morozzi knows she isn't in any condition to do much talking."

"But Bossy," Eve said wearily. She shivered. "It isn't over yet, Tom. They'll figure out Bossy was in your house—before Anitra was."

"They won't," I said quickly, "if Anitra can't talk to disprove it. We can't prove it. We wouldn't if we could."

The arrival of the V-8 cut off any more talk.

The Federal men were at the courthouse when we got there. Bart locked Mrs. Morozzi up and Sarakinnen gave her a sedative.

I came in to see the Federal men shaking hands with Dirkson. He looked at me. "All right, Hallam, will you stop suspecting me now?"

"I will," I said doggedly, "if you'll explain a few things. Why you tried to put me on the spot the first time you saw me. Why you claimed to have those clothes as evidence against me."

He grinned at that. "I had been hanging around for some time before I registered at the hotel here. I had things about ready to break—getting close to your Prigwell just as you figured it out. He knew the heat was on and was willing to take a chance on getting a short sentence. We didn't have enough proof to get him on the old blackmailing charges." He glanced at Eve but turned away quickly. He didn't allude to it again.

"When I had him that close," Dirkson went on, "I registered as Ralph Burnham at the hotel. I had Prigwell identification in my pockets. I was going to force Anitra's and Raymond's hands. They didn't know me—yet, and I was playing for them to break along with Prigwell.

"But they were too tough."

"He died," I interjected.

Dirkson grinned again. "You have strong theories, Hallam—they sound that way." I knew then Bossy would be all right, but I never did know whether she had convinced Adam she hadn't killed Prigwell or whether he knew and had lied to me about it.

Dirkson was talking again. "I had you lined up because I'd heard part of the marriage gag discussed when I was listening in on them. I was going to get around to you later, but you happened to be there when the sheriff was hauling me into jail. I took a chance on fingering you then. You showed me up easily enough as a liar, but it did call your attention to Saarkinnen. That helped me out."

"And the clothes?" I reminded him.

"I didn't get them," he admitted. "But I had seen them at your place and I was letting you know it would be smart to stay in line."

"I couldn't reconcile you and the things you did," I said to him.

One of the Federal men smiled at that. "You never can—that's why he takes this kind of job."

I nodded and went to where Eve was sitting. She was shivering a little. Saarkinnen was patting her gently. "It's all over, Eve, honey. All over."

Bart made comforting sounds in his throat. "The first one you shoot's the toughest, Eve," he said consolingly. He surveyed the group with placid eyes and then pulled a jug of whiskey from his desk. No one refused when he offered it around. We were damned glad to get it.

I felt better after the drink and Eve stopped quivering. A little color came back into her face. I gave her a cigarette and had one myself, feeling I'd earned it plenty, and said, "Is Prigwell really Prigwell? And how did he come by that identification as Ralph Burnham?"

"It's funny," Dirkson told us, "but he realty was Ralph Burnham. Only used the name Prigwell. Miss Vinson was right. Anitra—Irma, her name was—masqueraded as Burnham and passed for him as far as the public was concerned. It made for a nicely confusing set-up."

"How did you spot the connection?" Dirkson asked me.

"Eve did," I said. "Just before you nearly caught us in Anitra and Raymond what's-his-name's hotel rooms."

"Raymond Parkman, darling," Eve corrected automatically. She smiled a little.

"Parkman," I said dutifully. "Anyway, she found a razor with black hair in it. Now both Anitra and Raymond are blond. But at the time I didn't know whether to connect the hairs with you or the corpse, Dirkson. The fact is I found a size 34 suit in Raymond's closet and a small-sized hat. They would have fit you as well as Prigwell. I chose you—for a while."

Saarkinnen spoke up. "We have those silk hose as evidence for you, Dirkson, but if you didn't get the clothes and Anitra didn't get them, where are they?"

Eve flushed and smiled faintly. "I know that answer," she said. "Bossy is really quite naive. She took them— because she thought they were pretty and wanted them for me."

The Federal men grinned tolerantly at that. Bossy was in the clear as far as they were concerned. Eve was feeling better, too, and that perked her up a lot.

"We can't do much more'n get your statements. And Mrs. Morozzi's when she comes out of it," Saarkinnen said. "We'll get yours later," he added to Eve and me.

"I want to go home and get some sleep," Eve said.

"Sleep?" Saarkinnen's glance was surprised but his

tone was insinuating. "Sleep—now?"

"Certainly," Eve retorted. She smiled at him and tucked her arm in mine. "Do you want us to be tired tonight?"

THE END

Resurrected Press Books in *The Chief Inspector Pointer Mystery* Series

The Eames-Erskine Case (1924)
The Charteris Mystery (1925)
The Footsteps that Stopped (1926)
The Clifford Affair (1927)
The Cluny Problem (1928)
The Net Around Joan Ingilby (1928)
The Murder at the Nook (1929)
The Mysterious Partner (1929)
The Craig Poisoning Mystery (1930)
The Wedding Chest Mystery (1930)
The Upfold Farm Mystery (1931)
Death of John Tait (1932)
The Westwood Mystery (1932)
The Tall House Mystery (1933)
The Cautley Conundrum (1934)
The Paper-Chase (1934)
The Case of the Missing Diary (1935)
Tragedy at Beechcroft (1935)
The Case of the Two Pearl Necklaces (1935)
Mystery at the Rectory (1936)
Black Cats Are Lucky (1937)
Scarecrow (1937)
Pointer to a Crime (1944)

RESURRECTED PRESS BOOKS IN H. ASHBOOK'S
DETECTIVE SPIKE TRACY MYSTERY SERIES

The Murder of Cicely Thane (1930)

The Murder of Stephen Kester (1931)

The Murder of Sigurd Sharon (1933)

A Most Immoral Murder (1935)

Murder Makes Murder (1937)

Murder Comes Back (1940)

Murder on Friday (1941)

RESURRECTED PRESS BOOKS FROM *THE JAMES "BONNIE" DUNDEE MYSTERY* SERIES BY ANNE AUSTIN

The Black Pigeon

The Avenging Parrot

Murder Backstairs

Murder at Bridge

One Drop of Blood

Murdered, But Not Dead

AVAILABLE FROM RESURRECTED PRESS!

JOURNEYS INTO MYSTERY

A collection of three novels of travel and mystery from some of the best known writers of the Edwardian Age

A man is mysteriously murdered on the night express from Rome to Paris. Which one of the passengers is the murderer. The Countess? The General? The clergyman? The maid who disappeared?

A sapphire necklace stolen from a cab in the London fog. A ship's steward who is either more or less than he appears to be. A jewel thief who criss-crosses the Atlantic in search of victims.

A grand London hotel. A missing German prince. A murdered man whose body disappears from the hotel. These are the challenges facing an American millionaire and his daughter after he buys The Grand Babylon Hotel.

- **The Rome Express – Arthur Griffiths**

- **The Voice in the Fog – Harold MacGrath**

- **The Grand Babylon Hotel – Arnold Bennett**

- The Knight's Cross Signal Problem by Ernest Bramah
- The Problem of Cell 13 by Jacques Futrelle
- The Conundrum of the Golf Links by Percy James Brebner
- The Silkworms of Florence by Clifford Ashdown
- The Gateway of the Monster by William Hope Hodgson
- The Affair at the Semiramis Hotel by A. E. W. Mason
- The Affair of the Avalanche Bicycle & Tyre Co., LTD by Arthur Morrison

RESURRECTED PRESS CLASSIC MYSTERY CATALOGUE

Journeys into Mystery
Travel and Mystery in a More Elegant Time

The Edwardian Detectives
Literary Sleuths of the Edwardian Era

Gems of Mystery
Lost Jewels from a More Elegant Age

E. C. Bentley
Trent's Last Case: The Woman in Black

Ernest Bramah
Max Carrados Resurrected:
The Detective Stories of Max Carrados

Agatha Christie
The Secret Adversary
The Mysterious Affair at Styles

Octavus Roy Cohen
Midnight

Freeman Wills Croft
The Ponson Case
The Pit Prop Syndicate

J. S. Fletcher
The Herapath Property
The Rayner-Slade Amalgamation
The Chestermarke Instinct
The Paradise Mystery
Dead Men's Money

The Middle of Things
Ravensdene Court
Scarhaven Keep
The Orange-Yellow Diamond
The Middle Temple Murder
The Tallyrand Maxim
The Borough Treasurer
In the Mayor's Parlour
The Saftey Pin

R. Austin Freeman
*The Mystery of 31 New Inn from the Dr. Thorndyke
Series*
*John Thorndyke's Cases from the Dr. Thorndyke
Series*
The Red Thumb Mark from The Dr. Thorndyke Series
The Eye of Osiris from The Dr. Thorndyke Series
A Silent Witness from the Dr. John Thorndyke Series
The Cat's Eye from the Dr. John Thorndyke Series
*Helen Vardon's Confession: A Dr. John Thorndyke
Story*
As a Thief in the Night: A Dr. John Thorndyke Story
*Mr. Pottermack's Oversight: A Dr. John Thorndyke
Story*
*Dr. Thorndyke Intervenes: A Dr. John Thorndyke
Story*
The Singing Bone: The Adventures of Dr. Thorndyke
The Stoneware Monkey: A Dr. John Thorndyke Story
*The Great Portrait Mystery, and Other Stories: A
Collection of Dr. John Thorndyke and Other Stories*
The Penrose Mystery: A Dr. John Thorndyke Story
The Uttermost Farthing: A Savant's Vendetta

Arthur Griffiths
The Passenger From Calais
The Rome Express

Fergus Hume
The Mystery of a Hansom Cab
The Green Mummy
The Silent House
The Secret Passage

Edgar Jepson
The Loudwater Mystery

A. E. W. Mason
At the Villa Rose

A. A. Milne
The Red House Mystery
Baroness Emma Orczy
The Old Man in the Corner

Edgar Allan Poe
The Detective Stories of Edgar Allan Poe

Arthur J. Rees
The Hampstead Mystery
The Shrieking Pit
The Hand In The Dark
The Moon Rock
The Mystery of the Downs

Mary Roberts Rinehart
Sight Unseen and The Confession

Dorothy L. Sayers
Whose Body?

Sir William Magnay
The Hunt Ball Mystery

Mabel and Paul Thorne
The Sheridan Road Mystery

Louis Tracy
The Strange Case of Mortimer Fenley
The Albert Gate Mystery
The Bartlett Mystery
The Postmaster's Daughter
The House of Peril
The Sandling Case: What Would You Have Done?
Charles Edmonds Walk
The Paternoster Ruby

John R. Watson
The Mystery of the Downs
The Hampstead Mystery

Edgar Wallace
The Daffodil Mystery
The Crimson Circle

Carolyn Wells
Vicky Van
The Man Who Fell Through the Earth
In the Onyx Lobby
Raspberry Jam
The Clue
The Room with the Tassels
The Vanishing of Betty Varian
The Mystery Girl
The White Alley
The Curved Blades
Anybody but Anne
The Bride of a Moment
Faulkner's Folly
The Diamond Pin
The Gold Bag
The Mystery of the Sycamore
The Come Backy

Raoul Whitfield
Death in a Bowl

And much more!
Visit ResurrectedPress.com
for our complete catalogue

About Resurrected Press

A division of Intrepid Ink, LLC, Resurrected Press is dedicated to bringing high quality, vintage books back into publication. See our entire catalogue and find out more at www.ResurrectedPress.com.

For announcements and updates on upcoming publications, LIKE us on Facebook!

www.Facebook.com/ResurrectedPress